TALES BEYOND
MIDNIGHT

OTHER TITLES BY KIM GRAVELL

The Dark Places Novels

The Demon's Call

Child of the Covenant

To Pay for the Crossing

TALES BEYOND
MIDNIGHT
SHORT STORIES FOR SLEEPLESS NIGHTS

KIM GRAVELL

Published by Kim Gravell.

www.kimgravell.com

British Library Cataloguing in Publication Data.
A catalogue record for this book is available from the British Library.

Cover design by 100 Covers

ISBN 978 1916324 725

As an author, one of the most satisfying things a reader can tell me is that they have stayed awake into the early hours of the morning, unable to put my book down and desperate to find out what happens next.

This book is for everyone who has experienced sleepless nights because of my writing.

Thank you.

CONTENTS

1

JUMPER

'It's a long way down, mate.'

The voice coming out of the darkness was startling and he jerked involuntarily, his grip loosening on the rain-slicked safety rail. For a moment he scrabbled frantically, cold-numbed fingers unable to find a purchase on the wet metal, feet slipping on the scant three inches of ledge that was all that prevented him pitching out into the darkness. He was going to fall— then his hands closed once more around the top of the safety barrier and he clung to it, heart hammering, knees weak. Stupid really, that the thought of falling could still scare him, given what he intended to do. It was just that – well, he was going to jump, but it had to be deliberate, when he was ready, not because some idiot woman had startled him into letting go.

He shuffled his feet on the ledge, inching round until he was facing her, and glared over the barrier. He had a vague impression of having seen her from the corner of his eye, a dark shape coalescing out of the drizzle and the night as though she had had no existence before she had materialised here and spoken to him. A fanciful notion for a woman who, now he looked more closely, appeared so ordinary. Ankle boots and skinny jeans topped by a nondescript coat; rain-dampened mousy brown hair scraped back into a short ponytail away from a face which was bare of makeup. Not even a police officer – just an inconvenient housewife out for a late-night stroll.

'Stay away from me.'

'Sure. No problem.' The woman shrugged slim shoulders but made no other move, neither towards him nor away. Instead, she said, 'I'm Lucy,' and then, 'That's Luci with an I,' as though it could be of any conceivable interest to him, how she spelled her name. Where did she think she was? Some pretentious dinner party?

'Piss off, Lucy.' If he could have pronounced a Y at the end of her name he would have done so.

The woman raised an eyebrow as though she had

heard the consonant anyway but all she said was, 'What's your name?'

'It doesn't matter.'

'Of course it matters.' Then she corrected herself. 'No. Actually, you're right. It doesn't.' She was quiet for a moment and then, 'Hugo,' she said.

'What?'

'Hugo. You look like a Hugo.'

'Who the fuck looks like a Hugo?' Somehow, he found himself feeling offended.

'You do. Hugos are people who hold on tight to what's dear to them. Like you're doing right now. People who believe in something so much they're willing to die for it. Like you are. That's quite something. Not everyone has that much conviction.'

'Are you trying to make me feel good about chucking myself off a bridge?'

'What if I was? Would it be such a bad thing if it meant that you died happy?'

'I'll still be dead, won't I?'

'Yes, yes you will, and when I read about it in the paper I'll find out your real name. Then I'll say, "Oh, I knew him as Hugo. It's such a shame. He seemed like a nice man."'

'I'm not.'

'What, called Hugo? No, I know you're not.'

'I'm not a nice man. Nice men don't do what I did.'

Luci pulled a face but shied away from asking the obvious question. 'So, what are you called?'

She stood there on the correct side of the safety barrier, her head tilted to one side like an inquisitive blackbird, waiting for his response.

'God, you don't give up, do you?' he snarled under his breath but somehow found himself adding, 'If you must know, my name's David.'

Of all possible reactions her bright smile was probably the last he would have expected.

'David. That's nice. It means "beloved". Some would say, "beloved of God". Do you believe in God, David?'

'You're not going to preach at me, are you?'

For some reason that seemed to amuse her.

'No, that's hardly my department. Not many people do believe in God these days,' Luci continued as though his comment had answered her question. 'I think that's a shame.'

'What, life after death and all that stuff?' David eyed her scornfully. 'Come off it. Once you're dead, you're dead. That's it. The end. Finito.'

That earned him another eyebrow raise.

'Well, I guess you're going to find out soon enough, aren't you.' Her expression morphed into a wicked grin rendered less than human by the glare of the mercury lights high up on the arching ironwork of the bridge. 'D'you know something David? Suicides don't make much of a splash in the papers, but I reckon,' Luci paused and peered meaningfully over the safety rail, looking down into the darkness as though she could see through it to the swirling waters of the river below, 'you'll make one hell of a splash down there.'

In that moment David hated her. The strength of the feeling surprised him. He had thought himself numb. 'What do you care?'

Luci shoved her hands into the pockets of her coat. 'Maybe I don't. It seems such a waste, that's all. So, what did you do, David? What was so terrible that the best thing you can think of doing with your life now is ending it?'

'I—' He caught himself. Was he really going to tell some busybody do-gooder what he hadn't been able to share with his friends, his family? His breath huffed out in a short laugh, taking him by surprise. It seemed he was.

'I had – have – a gambling problem. I lost ... well, it doesn't matter how much. It was a lot of money. When my family found out I told them I was getting help. But I didn't. I just needed that one big win to sort things out, so I stole money from work to tide me over, to cover things up until—' He stopped and took a conscious breath, forcing back the tide of words. 'I was stupid.' He could see that now, but the knowledge didn't stop the temptation prickling at him, the awful burning surety that his luck would have changed, that it could still change if he stayed in the game.

'And now you've been found out?'

Luci's voice pulled him back.

'Not yet. But I will be. There's a company audit starting tomorrow. They'll find the money's missing and then that's me finished. I'll lose my job. They'll take my house. I'll go to prison and my wife ends up on the street.'

'So instead, you're going to kill yourself?'

'I can't stop!' There – he had said it. 'What else can I do?'

'You could start by talking to your boss before the audit. It seems to me that they abolished the death penalty for theft some time ago.'

'What good will that do? I'll still end up in prison.'

'Maybe you will. But you'll also get help. You've taken the first step by admitting to yourself that you have a problem. Now you need to be brave enough to tell the people who can do something about it, to ask for help and to take it when it's offered. Go to your boss. Confess. It will look much better than waiting to be found out.'

'My family will never speak to me again.'

'Well, they certainly won't be able to if you kill

yourself,' Luci said, bluntly. More gently she added, 'Whether they do or they don't, that's their decision. Don't make it for them. That's the coward's way out and I think you're better than that, David.'

For a moment David eyed the young woman who had taken the time to stand in the cold and the dark, literally talking him down from the precipice. It felt as though the night had closed in around them. He was no longer aware of the orange glow from the streetlights in the old town or the black silhouettes of the power station cooling towers looming at his back. No traffic sounds filtered through the damp midnight air and even the stars had faded. It seemed as though he and Luci were cut out of time, separated from reality. In that space he could pause for long enough to envisage his life taking a different turn.

'Do you really think so?'

'I do. Come on now, get back over this railing.'

David swallowed hard and then nodded a silent okay, reaching instinctively towards the hand she extended. The hand that grabbed his shoulder as he moved forward and gave a single hard shove.

'Oops!'

Luci leaned a little way over the safety rail and looked down to where the scream had ended. 'Oh yes. Just as I thought: one hell of a splash.'

She allowed herself a satisfied smile. That was the thing about collecting damned souls: it was so much sweeter if you could get them to change their minds at the last minute and decide – just a little too late – that they'd rather live.

'We'll discuss this later, David. You and I. We'll have all the time in the world.'

Still smiling she turned and walked away into the darkness, her footsteps clip-clip-clipping like the sound of dainty cloven hooves on the wet pavement.

ABOUT 'JUMPER'

The setting for this story is the Runcorn Widnes bridge – the 'old' bridge, that is, rather than the Mersey Gateway Bridge that opened in 2017. The power station mentioned towards the end is Fiddler's Ferry. Long since decommissioned now, demolition of its cooling towers started in 2023. However, when I first conceived this piece, they were a well-known and prominent feature of the local landscape.

I toyed with various scenarios for this story: the standard Good Samaritan tale, perhaps with the jumper returning to the bridge, after a spell in prison, in the hope of re-encountering their saviour; or one where the

Samaritan turned out to be the ghost of someone who hadn't been talked out of jumping. Such options felt too obvious and I eventually settled on this version with a sting in its twisted tail.

The line, 'Oops!' makes some people laugh. Are you one of them?

2

FAMILY PLANNING

I'm going to take the pill tomorrow. I've decided. Daniel thought it was a bad idea, but he's not here to stop me now so it's my choice. When the first video campaigns were shown he got angry. He said it wasn't our job to solve the problem, that overpopulation was just something we were going to have to live with. He said the scientists should come up with some other solution, that something like the pill was just plain wrong.

I pretended to agree. I didn't want us to fight. I think of us lying in bed together at night, the smell of his skin, the feel of his body next to mine … but after we'd made love, when he'd fall asleep, holding me in his arms, my head cradled on his chest, I'd lie awake and I'd worry. How could we dare to bring another child into the world? We all know that there isn't enough to go around. There are too many people and not enough food. It doesn't take a genius to work out that something has to be done.

I'd think of Bethan, lying in her crib. The thought of her going hungry made me want to cry. Of course, she never did. Daniel was good like that. I know he went short to make sure that Bethan and I had enough. He thought I didn't notice because I didn't say anything – what woman could berate her husband for going without so that his wife and daughter didn't? – but over the months I felt the flesh over his ribs grow thinner and my heart ached for him as much as for our baby girl. I would try and slip bits from my plate onto his but he'd say that he was full and push his plate away, patting his stomach and saying what a great cook I was to make such wonderful meals and how good they made him feel. Then he'd insist that I ate the leftovers because it would be criminal to waste them.

Everyone over sixteen is being encouraged to take the pill. There's a clinic at the local hospital. All I need to do is go down there and register. I've seen it in the videos. There are some forms to fill in, then they'll scan my identity chip so that my decision is recorded in the system. After that they'll give me the pill. It's all very simple. You can see that they're trying to make it as easy as possible for people.

But Daniel was adamant that it was wrong. The government doesn't have the right to force that kind of decision on people, he'd say. You don't see the ministers queueing up to register, do you? But you do. You see them, on the news videos. Some of them were the first to volunteer. When I said that, Daniel laughed and told me not to be so naïve. Did I really think they took it? Of course I did, you could see them on the videos. Daniel said that was a scam, that the pills the officials took had all been doctored, that they weren't real. But I think they were. I believe.

The population is too big. There's no argument there. People are starving and taking the pill is the best option for us. We have to reduce the population size. Daniel said he'd divorce me if I took the pill. I told him not to be silly, that I'd be doing it for him and for Bethan, but he still didn't agree.

The thing is, if you take it – even if it doesn't work – the government will guarantee you'll get full rations, just because you were willing to do your bit. I could share mine with Daniel and Bethan, so we would all be better off. And if it did work then Bethan would be guaranteed full rations for life and a place in the best school and a job at the end of her education. It would be worth it to ensure our little girl had a good life, but Daniel didn't agree with me. He said it was wrong, that the scientists and the government were playing God, trying to make us take it.

How would they know, he said, when enough people had taken it? How would they balance the population? Things have gone wrong in the past when governments have tried to intervene like this. Think of the problems in the 21st Century, back when there was foetal selection based on sex.

When it started everyone thought it was a marvellous idea; families could opt to have boys instead of girls. And of course they did. The thing was that too many people opted to have only boys and too few girls were born. No one thought it was a problem until they started to realise that there weren't enough women to go around. All those young men with no hope of having a wife or a family of their own. First there was violence and civil unrest but eventually there were wars. I remember reading about them in school. They lasted into the 22nd Century. All that bloodshed because governments thought they knew best.

I tried to explain to Daniel that the pill wasn't like that. It was balanced they said. It would work in fifty percent of the people who took it but it would be random. You wouldn't know until you took it if you were one of the ones who would be affected. That way everyone could be sure that there was no ulterior plan. It was fair;

everyone had the same chance. So, the more people who could be encouraged to take it the better. Hence the incentives in terms of increased rations if you volunteered, regardless of whether or not it worked.

But Daniel said no. That was when he started to get involved in the food riots. He argued that the government could do more to distribute rations equally. He said that the ministers were hoarding food for their families while the people on the streets went hungry. Protesting was the only way to make it right, he said. But the protests were heavily policed and they were getting increasingly violent. I told him not to go. I begged him, but he said it was the only way. I knew it was only a matter of time before something happened and he didn't come back and I was right.

I couldn't believe it at first. Every time someone came to the door I'd look up, thinking it had to be him; but it never was. Even after the police came and told me he'd been identified by his chip, I didn't want to believe. It would have helped if I'd been allowed to see his body but by the time I was notified it had already been taken away to one of the lime pits. They couldn't tell me which one.

That was a month ago. Bethan and I still get our rations. Even though Daniel was classified as an enemy of the state for joining in the riots, it didn't affect us. The government is fair like that. But now I'm going to bed hungry at night so that Bethan doesn't. I can see my ribs now, just as I could see Daniel's and I know I'm going to have to do something.

So, first thing tomorrow I'm going to go down to the clinic. I'll leave Bethan with Michaela, our next door neighbour. She won't mind looking after her for a few hours. When I sign the forms I'll let them know where she is so that, if it works, the authorities will come and get her. Of course, it will be hard, leaving her behind, but I've made my mind up. It's the best thing I can do for my daughter.

On the videos it all looks so peaceful. Once you've registered, they take you through to the ward. There are beds there, lovely soft ones with proper blankets and pillows. You take the pill they give you and then you lie down. The people on the video just closed their eyes. They looked as though they had gone to sleep. There were eight of them: four men and four women. Different races, different ages, to show that everyone should get involved, that the program is for everyone. They all lay down on those lovely soft beds and went to sleep. The first time I saw the video I cried when it showed the people the pill had worked for. They looked so peaceful, so noble. Two men and two women out of that group of eight. Daniel said that proved the video was fixed. He said if the pill was random then it wouldn't have worked like that. Statistics weren't that neat, he said. I understood what he meant but I didn't agree.

Anyway, now I've decided. Tomorrow it will be me taking the pill and lying down on one of those beds. They say they're going to put up statues to honour the people who've joined in the scheme, the ones who've acted to help save the rest of the population. It's a nice thought that my name might be on one of them, but that's not why I'm doing it. I'm doing it because taking that pill will guarantee my daughter a better life. Still, I can't help but wonder if I'll be one of the ones it works for: the fifty percent who die. I only hope it's not painful.

ABOUT 'FAMILY PLANNING'

The unchecked growth of the human population is the elephant in the room when we talk about man-made threats to our planet's future. Bond villains and other megalomaniacs might plan to deal with the problem by wiping out a percentage of the population – selecting for specific traits or choosing them at random according to the whims of the scriptwriter. I wondered how we might address the situation in a voluntary way.

3

NOW WHAT?

Was this really what it was like to be dead? Seriously? Watching the aftermath of the accident unfolding around her, Lizzy was unimpressed. What about the loved ones who had died before her? Shouldn't they be here to greet her, to guide her on to whatever it was that the afterlife held in store? She looked around again but there were no familiar faces amongst the bystanders, no one to explain what happened next. At the very least, she thought, there should have been a bright light she was meant to go towards. Shouldn't there?

But there was nothing. Feeling lost she wandered across to the paramedic bent over what she supposed was still her body.

'Don't bother, mate. I'm dead.'

He continued with his examination although, from the angle of her neck, it must have been obvious she was beyond any help he could offer. She had had barely a second to register the car pulling out in front of her before she and her bike had collided with it. The best cycling helmet money could buy hadn't been enough to save her.

Self-consciously Lizzy put her hand to her neck. It felt alright and, when she tried, she couldn't turn her head any further than she had been able to when she was alive. That was good, she decided. She wouldn't like to go through the afterlife with her head flopping to one side or turned so she was facing backwards.

But what was she meant to do? A serious-looking police officer had joined the paramedic and Lizzy shivered as she heard the word 'morgue' mentioned. She didn't like the sound of that. Morgues were cold, clinical places. Not that she had ever been in one but that was the image she had from television. If she was meant to stay with her body she didn't want it to be somewhere like that. But did she have to? She realised she no longer felt any attachment to the sad remains the paramedic had just covered with a blanket. The body had been her – but it wasn't any longer. She refocused when the police officer mentioned the car driver.

'He doesn't need any help,' she muttered, crossly. He'd been safe in his metal shell when he'd driven out in front of her. There had been no chance of him ending up lying dead in the middle of the road. A surge of anger washed through her. There he was, still sat in his car, another police officer talking to him through the open door.

'She came out of nowhere. She was going so fast I didn't see her.'

'You didn't see me because you didn't bother to look!'

The policeman took no notice of Lizzy but the driver jerked as if slapped. 'What? What did you say?'

'I didn't say anything, sir. You were telling me what happened.'

'And I'm telling you what actually happened,' Lizzy snapped.

The driver's eyes darted round. 'She's here, isn't she? I can hear her.'

'Have you been drinking, sir?'

Intrigued Lizzy peered round the policeman. 'Can you see me as well?' she asked her killer.

His scream gave her all the answer she needed. 'She's there! Oh, dear God! She's there! Keep her away from me!'

Behind her the ambulance left but Lizzy felt no

compunction to go with it. This was far more satisfying. She pulled a ghastly face and stepped closer to the driver who cowered backwards, waving his hands frantically in an attempt to ward her off. For the first time since her death Lizzy relaxed. Now she knew just what she was going to do with her afterlife. She was going to be a ghost!

ABOUT 'NOW WHAT?'

A short piece prompted by the coming together of a loved one on a bike and an inattentive car driver pulling out from a junction. Fortunately, no ghosts were created as a result.

4

RAINBOW LADY AND THE BONE FAIRY

'This one is mean.'

The Bone Fairy jerked her chin at the man sat on the opposite side of the room and hissed at him through her bared teeth. Rainbow Lady glanced at her companion in surprise. It wasn't that the Bone Fairy had volunteered an unsolicited opinion – though guardian spirits weren't supposed to do so she had long since accepted that the Bone Fairy had her own rules on such things. No, what interested the healer was the tone in which that viewpoint had been expressed. Not much upset the Bone Fairy but this man's presence had.

'I don't like him.'

'You don't have to like me, Sweet Cheeks.'

The words and the accompanying leer were obviously meant to offend, and the Bone Fairy's reaction was sadly predictable. While Rainbow Lady would have opted for a cool stare, rather than give the speaker the satisfaction of knowing he had annoyed her, once roused the Bone Fairy did not believe in hiding her feelings. She hissed again, her body rearing up, her arms spreading out like a cobra's hood. The man's fists clenched and he leaned forward, his jaw jutting out provocatively. Had it not been for the body of the woman stretched between them the two might have come to blows.

'Enough!' Rainbow Lady's voice rang through the darkened room. 'Neither of you has to like the other. That's not why we're here.'

'Then why are we here? What right have you to summon me?' The man sneered but the contempt in his voice didn't quite cover his annoyance at being brought here against his will. Rainbow Lady's invocation had been strong enough to bind him and that rankled deeply.

'I think we should ask her.' Rainbow Lady nodded at the woman lying between the two spirits. With her closed eyes and peaceful expression she might have been sleeping. She was, in fact, in a deep trance.

Her given name was Miriam, but she was known by many in the valley as Scared of Thunder. She had turned up one afternoon the previous spring, walking through the dust on the narrow path that led in from the broken lands, bringing with her no more than one small, spotted pony could drag on a travois and the clothes on her back. She gave no reason for coming to the valley, nor for wanting to stay. She simply found a family willing to give her lodgings and settled in, setting up a small workshop for it turned out that she was a skilled weaver of grasses and willow. The baskets she created were practical and tightly woven but also beautiful, the intertwining textures of their sides giving as much pleasure to the hands as their subtly blended colours did to the eyes. Rainbow Lady had several of them in her own home.

It was only when the storm season came and Miriam was found quaking in the corn cellar at the first sign of rain-clouds that her peculiar phobia had become known. Instead of celebrating the coming of the storms and the rumbling visitations of the Ones Who Drum Thunder, Miriam was terrified of them. No one could understand why. While her new neighbours tried to overlook this peculiarity – for in all other respects the woman was an asset to the valley – it wasn't long before the name coined by the children had gained a wider usage. As the year rolled round, and the late summer storms were nearly upon them once more, Miriam had sought Rainbow Lady's help.

Rainbow Lady picked up her tortoiseshell rattle, offering it briefly to each of the six directions. Then she shook it over supine woman's chest. 'Miriam, come and join us.'

She sent out her summons confidently, secure in the knowledge that the circle she had cast would protect against any malign interference. She had closed it as soon as she had conjured the spirit she had felt bound to Miriam – that of the man currently sat opposite the Bone Fairy. Nothing else could enter. Nor could anything leave without her permission – a condition that was surely responsible for some of the sullen anger radiating from the male spirit. Rainbow Lady acknowledged the emotion but was unconcerned by it.

'Miriam,' she called again and, in the space between one heartbeat and the next, a new presence coalesced in the shadows just beyond Miriam's head.

Rainbow Lady's eyebrows rose slightly at the sight. The shape Miriam's spirit had chosen wasn't that of the woman she was now. Instead, this was a young girl of some five or six summers. Blonde hair, bleached almost white by the sun, framed a freckled face. Wide eyes, the blue-green of the precious turquoise which was sometimes found in the hills, stared back at her, direct and guileless and without fear.

'Hello.' The Bone Fairy spoke before the healer could do so. 'You must be Miriam. You should come and sit with me.' She opened her arms and, to Rainbow Lady's surprise, Miriam climbed unhesitatingly into the spirit's lap.

Now that was unusual. Of the few people who encountered the Bone Fairy, most were extremely wary of her. Rainbow Lady supposed it was down to her guardian spirit's appearance.

At first glance the Bone Fairy looked like a beautiful young woman with high cheekbones, green eyes and long caramel-coloured hair – uncommon among the residents of the valley – which flowed down to her knees in dozens of intertwining braids. Yet there was something about her that made people uneasy, something which the brain would prefer not to register, which it made the eyes skip over. Something about her wasn't quite right. And then people would realise just what it was that they were trying not to see. The Bone Fairy had no nose. Rainbow Lady had asked her about this once. 'Skulls don't have noses,' had been the reply. Skulls didn't have tongues either, but this had never troubled the Bone Fairy who could be very talkative when she felt like it.

Fingers were something else the Bone Fairy

struggled with. Her fingertips – and sometimes entire digits – appeared as bone, although regardless of how they looked they invariably felt like warm human fingers, properly enclosed in flesh. They had when they had clamped around Rainbow Lady's wrist, the first time they had met, many, many moons ago, soft and warm but inhumanly strong. Rainbow Lady sometimes wondered how the Bone Fairy's toes would appear, but she had never seen them. To her eyes at least the spirit's feet were always clad in soft doeskin boots with exquisitely detailed beading winding up around her calves.

Watching Miriam settle into the Bone Fairy's lap, Rainbow Lady wondered what the child was seeing; if she imagined she saw a pert nose or if there was just a black void in the face above her.

Either way the view didn't seem to bother the girl. She looked up at the Bone Fairy and laughed – a delightful, frivolous sound. 'You're pretty.'

The Bone Fairy preened – Rainbow Lady had long known her friend was susceptible to flattery – and shook a handful of her braids playfully in the child's face. Miriam giggled and Rainbow Lady swallowed a small sigh. It was a beguiling picture but ...

'If we might continue.'

The Bone Fairy's wide, rather generous mouth, formed briefly into a little moue of irritation but the healer felt the spirit's focus come back to her and the task in hand.

'Tell us what happened, Miriam.'

The girl looked at Rainbow Lady, her eyes saucer-wide, then shot a pleading look at the Bone Fairy.

'It's alright, little one.' The Bone Fairy smiled at the child. 'You can tell us. Whatever it was, we won't mind.'

Miriam bit her lower lip as though she didn't quite believe this, but the Bone Fairy tapped her gently under the chin and, after a moment, she nodded. 'He took it from me.' She looked accusingly at the man sat opposite her.

He snorted and rolled his eyes. 'Yeah, like she'd have anything that I'd want.'

The Bone Fairy shot him a withering glance over the blonde head then turned her attention back to Miriam. 'What did he take, little one?'

'The pearl.' The girl shrank into the Bone Fairy's lap as though she expected to be punished for this admission.

'She's crazy,' the man snarled, throwing his hands up in disgust. 'Do I look like I've got some kind of pearl?'

'We shall see.' Rainbow Lady cut off both further protest and the Bone Fairy's likely response. 'Show me,' she commanded in a voice of power.

Energy thrummed within the shielded circle. The air crackled, the pressure increasing until Rainbow Lady had to resist the urge to yawn to clear her throbbing ears. And then, there it was. Not a physical pearl but a beautiful multi-coloured orb of light, shimmering in the air just in front of the man's crossed feet.

Even without touching it Rainbow Lady could sense the power bound within that numinous shape. It called enticingly to her, the shifting pattern of colours drawing her gaze as though there was something hidden in their midst that she alone was meant to see. If she could just hold it … but no. Reluctantly she tore her eyes away, wondering at the object's power.

She turned to the child. 'Where did you get this, Miriam?'

'The Sky People gave it to me. They told me that one day I'd know how to use it and I had to keep it safe until then. But he took it—'

'She's lying,' the man spoke angrily across the child's hesitant voice. 'Okay, sure, I've got it, but so what? I didn't take it from her. She gave it to me.'

Rainbow Lady gave him a quelling look but she turned to the girl cuddled in the Bone Fairy's lap and asked carefully, 'Is this true Miriam? Did you give it to him?'

Miriam shook her head, but Rainbow Lady noted

that the girl didn't look at her when she answered.

'He heard I was having dreams and he guessed the Sky People were talking to me. He kept asking and asking what they'd given me. So, I told him about the pearl. I thought he might help me look after it.'

'She told me she didn't want it. She was scared and wanted me to take it away from her. When I asked her, she said I could keep it.'

'Miriam?'

'I didn't mean forever.' The little girl's voice quivered as she struggled against tears. 'I thought he could help me. But now the Sky People want to know what I've done with it and I can't tell them. I'm sorry.'

'Hush.' The Bone Fairy tucked Miriam's face against her chest, wrapping her arms protectively around the sobbing child and rocking her soothingly. She glared over the top of Miriam's head as Rainbow Lady studied the orb.

'This is a vision of great power. A healer's vision.' No wonder the child had been frightened of it and the man had coveted it for his own. Rainbow Lady folded her hands into her lap, resisting her own urge to reach for the sphere. With such power to call on ... but it wasn't for her to use, regardless of how much she might wish it were otherwise.

There was no doubt in her mind that Miriam's

Sky People were the Thunder Drummers, those elemental forces that manifested in the black clouds beyond the sunset. They were known for sharing wisdom through visions but they were not wholly benign. To have been granted such a gift and not to have used it was courting danger, but to have asked someone to take the vision away from her ... it certainly explained Miriam's fear of storms.

But what of the man who had done this? Rainbow Lady could sense the wards that still clung to the surface of the sphere. They were ugly and crude, sufficient to block an untrained mind, whether that of a child or the adult she would become, but with no hint of the finesse required to use a vision of this nature, even if that were possible when it was intended for another. Nor were the wards meant to fade with time. The fact that they had endured after the man's death told her as much.

Rainbow Lady weighed the man, reading what he would have been like when he was alive. She did not like what she found. 'You must have known what this vision was when you warded it. Why take it from her like that? It wasn't as though you could use it yourself. Yet even when you were dying you wouldn't release it.'

'Why should I have?'

'Because you should never have taken it from her. It wasn't yours to interfere with. This young girl was given a vision that would have turned her into a great healer, and you stole that from her. Not just from her, but from everyone she would have helped.' The enormity of that loss sliced across Rainbow Lady's senses. The sheer pointlessness of it hurt her. The man had gained nothing from binding the vision save the warped satisfaction of knowing no one else could make use of it. 'You have to give it back.'

'You can't make me.' The man's voice was sullen but there was defiance there too. His hands moved protectively to guard the glowing sphere.

'Is that what you believe?' Angered by his selfishness Rainbow Lady allowed a little of her own power to show in her aura, but the man was uncowed.

'She asked me to do it. She wanted shot of the vision and the dreams and I was willing to help her. If she's changed her mind that's too bad but you can't force me to hand over something I was asked to take.'

'She was a child. She didn't know what she was doing.'

'That doesn't matter.' The rough voice turned belligerent. 'She still asked me to take it from her so if you want me to release it there has to be a trade. You know it.'

And much though she would have liked to deny it, Rainbow Lady did. Miriam might not have known the consequences of what she was doing – she had been too young to understand and was frightened of the power being promised to her – but in the sacred space of the healing circle there was no escaping the fact that she had willingly asked for the vision to be taken away. Rainbow Lady sighed. She might wish it were different but that didn't make it so.

'Alright,' she conceded. There was no point in drawing the argument out. 'What do you want?'

'Hah!' The man shifted forward, a little bouncing movement of barely contained energy. 'I knew. I knew.' He hugged himself triumphantly as he rocked. 'You want it back so badly you're going to have to pay for it. Oh yes. Summoning me here, throwing your power around as though you have the right to command me. I know your type. You think you can have everything your own way, but you made a mistake this time. You made a mistake thinking you could order me around and now you have to pay.'

Rainbow Lady listened impassively letting the needling, gloating words pass her by without reaction, waiting for the man to come to the point.

'You said it right, there's power there. More power than you've got. Or you, Sweet Cheeks.' He sneered briefly at the Bone Fairy before locking his gaze back on Rainbow Lady. 'So, what's it worth, eh? That's the question. A vision as powerful as you say it is.' He looked at the healer greedily and the tip of his tongue slid over his lips as though already tasting the sweetness of his victory. A cruel light burned in his eyes. 'I'd say it's worth your life.'

'No!' The Bone Fairy hissed and would have risen but for the child in her lap. Rainbow Lady raised her hand in warning, backing up the gesture with a small slap of power, and the guardian spirit subsided, watching her with hurt and wary eyes. Satisfied she would not try to interfere Rainbow Lady turned back to the man, considering what he had said.

This was a vision of great power that would be returned to a woman not to a child. The child had been too young to accept it, but the woman ... Rainbow Lady had no doubt that Miriam would use her vision and that would be worth everything the man was asking. Her life? The healer smiled sadly to herself. For several moons she had been aware of the lump growing in her breast. She knew all too well what her future held. Perhaps if she could wield the vision for herself ... but she couldn't. The power it held wasn't intended for her but she could see it returned to the one who had been meant to use it. Her smile took on a fiercer edge. The bargain the man offered was no defeat: indeed, it might yet prove to be a mercy.

Rainbow Lady lifted her chin and regarded her adversary dispassionately, regal as a queen considering the granting of a favour. 'Alright.'

To her left the Bone Fairy's shocked whimper was the sound of an animal in pain.

Peace. The healer sent a warm tendril of affection towards her oldest friend. *I know what it is that I'm doing.*

'I accept.' But before the man could open his mouth to gloat, she continued, 'But you have kept this vision from being used for eighteen years and for that there must also be payment. A month for each year. That is what I claim from you.' Eighteen months: not long to train a successor and to pass on everything she knew, but perhaps long enough if she trusted in the Ones Who Drum Thunder's choice. 'After that my life is forfeit.'

Giving him no time to reconsider Rainbow Lady drew the ritual knife from her belt. 'Hold out your hand.' Placing her left hand beside his she drew the knife through the air above them. A slash of red appeared across both palms, morphing into a silvery white scar a moment later. 'The bargain is sealed. Miriam, you should take what is yours.'

From the safety of the Bone Fairy's lap Miriam held out her hands. The glowing vision sphere floated towards her and settled in her cupped palms.

'We will talk about this when you wake. Go back now.'

Silently the child stood and, as she did so she

changed, her form becoming that of the young woman lying in the centre of the circle. She bowed to Rainbow Lady and to the Bone Fairy, then she stepped towards the supine body on the floor and vanished.

The valley's healer stood on the high sandstone ridge, watching the sun sink the last few inches towards the horizon. As it touched the edge of the hills she raised her hand and blew the palmful of pollen she held onto the sunset wind.

> *In peace may you go, great blessings before you.*
> *In peace may you go, great blessings behind.*
> *In peace may you go, great blessings around you.*
> *In peace may you go, great blessings to find.*

She sang the words with her inner voice, filling them with love and sending them into the ether as both prayer and offering, just as she had been taught. Her teacher was gone now but she would honour her still.

For a moment longer she stood, watching the pollen grains dancing like motes of dust through the amber coloured light.

'She went so quickly.' She ran her hand over the simple wooden grave marker as she spoke. 'I tried everything she taught me, everything I knew to fight it. I almost dared to hope we were winning.' She turned to look at her companion, standing silently in the shadows of the ridgepole pines. 'But it was so quick at the end, so sudden. That last day she seemed so alive and then ...' Her hand grew still on the pale wood. 'Then she was gone.' That fact was still enough to shake her. In a quieter voice she continued, 'I've not seen a passing like that before. I'm sure she knew it was coming.'

'Perhaps she did, Miriam,' the Bone Fairy offered. 'Perhaps she did.'

ABOUT 'RAINBOW LADY AND THE BONE FAIRY'

As far back as I can remember I have felt an affinity with arid landscapes, from the dusty hills of the Middle East to the deserts and canyonlands of the American Midwest. Long before I had the opportunity to visit them, they felt familiar in a way I find hard to explain. It's a curious thing for a woman born and raised in England's green and pleasant land and who has chosen to live in the verdant – and frequently rain-blessed – countryside of mid-Wales.

In my mind the valley, where this story takes place, is in just such a desert area where the air is dry and smells of dust and the resiny sweetness of pine.

5

THE PSYCHIC

'It's mad cousin Daphne,' Mum announced, the moment I opened the door.

'And it's nice to see you too, Mum.'

She steamed past me, my sarcasm bouncing off her unnoticed, knocked aside like flotsam caught in the bow wave of a super-tanker.

Resigned, I followed her into the sitting room. 'What's she done this time?'

Mum dropped heavily onto the settee. 'She's been talking to the dead.'

Ah.

'But are they talking back?'

'Apparently Great Uncle Albert is.'

'Seriously? I wouldn't have thought he'd talk to her. He's been dead long enough to know the ropes.'

Mum gave me one of her looks. 'The timing of Great Uncle Albert's demise and the likelihood of him flouting the protocols is scarcely the point. The issue here is that Daphne has been doing things that she shouldn't. I want you to have a word with her. You're the only one she'll listen to.'

'Except Great Uncle Albert,' I muttered.

'What was that?'

'Nothing, Mum.'

'It's not just that it will reflect badly on the family. She'll get herself into all sorts of trouble. You know she's not a registered medium. What if the Council hear about it? They'll have her sectioned.'

Sectioned.

The word made my stomach twist because I knew Mum wasn't talking about the local borough council. She was referring to the Council of Ren: the frighteningly powerful body that controls those of us with psychic powers. When they spoke of sectioning, they didn't mean the cosy 'commit you to an asylum, under the Mental Health Act, and take good care of you' arrangement of the mundane world. Theirs was the 'cut into thin slices' variety of sectioning – often while the subject was still alive. Daphne might not be high on my list of favourite people, but I wouldn't wish that on anyone.

Here's the thing: those of us who can communicate with the dead don't. Or at least we don't go in for social calls and chit chat. We let the false mediums do that. The Council takes a hard line on cross-veil communications and for good reason: the dead don't like to be bothered. Think of it as diplomatic relations between two potentially hostile countries. You don't want any Tom, Dick or Daphne trying to muscle in and muddying the waters. You only want recognised channels of communication and those kept as limited as possible for fear of starting a war. Some of the dead can be – well – deadly when provoked and we try very hard not to provoke them.

But sometimes someone who's passed decides they want to communicate – stupidity isn't the sole prerogative of the living – and if they find an unregulated channel then things can get messy. Daphne is registered as a null. That's someone with the right blood lines to be able to communicate, but who can't. Yet now my mad cousin was and, even if she was only talking to relatives who should have known better, she was heading for trouble. The Council of Ren doesn't believe in reclassifying people, they just remove the discrepancy.

I sighed. What choice did I have? 'I'll go and talk

to her.'

So that was how I came to be standing outside Daphne's flat at number 2. Thornberry Avenue on a damp April afternoon. Normally I don't have much time for Daphne. She has a puddle where her brain should be, but that's no reason for her to be sectioned. Still, I wondered what I was going to be able to do about it.

Daphne opened the door on my third knock. The women in our family have a tendency towards being large. Big boned, Mum likes to call it. We're not necessarily fat but we're certainly statuesque. At five foot eight and a comfortable size 16 I'm regarded as the runt of the litter. Daphne was at the larger end of the family spectrum. In a floor-length floral kaftan, she looked like an explosion in the flower section of Smithfield market.

'Oh, Daphne.' I took in the henna-red hair escaping from beneath a bright turquoise turban and the gold hooped earrings. 'Tell me you're not—'

I got no further before I was crushed against her immense bosom in a patchouli-scented hug.

'Sal! Sal, it's marvellous. Oh, do come in and let me tell you about it.'

Before I could argue she had pulled me inside and bustled me into her living room. I thought it had acquired a few more crystal balls and mystical paraphernalia since

I had last visited. This wasn't a good sign.

'I've had a breakthrough, Sal, with my mediumship.'

'Yes, Mum told me. Are you sure about this, Daphne?'

'Oh, absolutely.'

Daphne's eyes were bright with enthusiasm. I wondered if she had been taking anything to help her clairvoyance. The Council would take a dim view of that, too.

'I've been hearing Great Uncle Albert.'

I winced. So, it was true.

'Or Al, as he likes to be known these days,' Daphne added with a delighted smile.

What?

I took a steadying breath, already regretting what I was going to say but knowing I had to get to the bottom of this. 'Why don't you tell me all about it?'

My cousin needed no further encouragement.

'Oh Sal, it all started when those nasty people from upstairs moved out. I knew they were polluting the ether: I just knew it. I did a full astral cleansing just as soon as they'd closed the front door. Anyway, once Mr and Mrs Constantine moved in, the whole atmosphere of the building lifted. I've not talked to them properly yet but I'm sure they must be deeply spiritual. It's the only explanation. The bad people move out, the good people move in, the etheric vibrations shift and all of a sudden I can hear them.'

'Them?' This was going from bad to worse. 'I thought it was only Great Uncle— no, never mind. Tell me how you first made contact.'

'Well, I was meditating in my favourite chair. I suppose I was a little tired and I slipped into a deeper trance than usual and that was when I heard the voices. It was Grandma Elsie. I'd know her voice anywhere with her Cockney accent. Bow Bells and all that, you remember how she was. It couldn't have been anyone else. Anyway, she was calling him.'

'Calling who?'

'Great Uncle Albert, of course. But it's like I said, now they're on the other side she calls him Al.'

I hadn't quite believed her the first time she had said it. In life, Great Uncle Albert had only ever been known as Great Uncle Albert – complete with the attendant capitalisation. The idea of him responding to any lesser epithet was hard to accept. The chorus of the Paul Simon song 'You can call me Al' popped into my mind. I pushed it away with a shudder.

'And this has just happened the once?' If we were lucky this had been a single aberration.

'Oh, no.' Daphne beamed delightedly. 'That's

what's so marvellous. It's every time I meditate. Of course, I can only hear them at the moment. I can't speak to them yet, or at least they don't respond to me, but I'm working on that. I'm sure with the way I've been improving it's only a matter of time.'

Daphne beamed again. I remembered how much she'd wanted to be a medium when we were growing up and how disappointed she'd been when her talents hadn't developed. But, even with such disappointment, she'd never shown any resentment towards my skills. The recollection softened my attitude towards her ... a little.

'Why don't you show me?'

Almost bouncing with delight, Daphne went over to the chair in the corner of the room. I should have known this was her special meditation chair by the large rose quartz pyramid which had been positioned on the seat and by the fluffy throw, festooned with stars and pentacles, draped over the back. Daphne removed the pyramid and carefully placed it on the floor in front of the chair, like an uncomfortable foot stool. She draped the throw over her shoulders and then settled herself down, shuffling her bulk around to get comfortable. Then, once she was satisfied, she closed her eyes and positioned her hands on her lap, palms uppermost and thumbs and forefingers touching in the traditional gesture beloved of yogis, spiritual practitioners and false mediums the world over.

But, instead of going into a trance, Daphne fell asleep. I could tell that by the way her head dropped back against the wall. That and she started snoring. I sat there for thirty increasingly boring minutes, watching her. In the end I got fed up and kicked her in the shin.

Daphne jerked, straightened up in the chair and looked around her. When her eyes lit on me she positively beamed. 'They were there, Sal, I heard them.'

It was hard to put a damper on such enthusiasm, but the threat of sectioning demanded that I do so. 'I'm not so sure, Daphne. Maybe you should tell me what you heard.'

'Well, it's as though I'm in the room with them, listening, while they have a conversation. Today they were talking about what they're going to have for tea. They're going to have crab sandwiches.'

I rolled my eyes. Trust my mad cousin to pick up on food.

Daphne carried on oblivious. 'Grandma Elsie was there and Great Uncle Albert was talking to someone he calls Glory. Isn't that wonderful?'

I wasn't sure about wonderful. Bizarre maybe.

'You're sure this started when the people upstairs moved in?' Could they be influencing Daphne in some way? Spiking the drinking water, perhaps? 'I think I'd better have a chat with them.'

I wasn't sure what I was going to be met with when I knocked on the door of the upstairs flat. What I got was a slightly plump, rather cheerful looking man, with grey hair and a brown cardigan, the sort with pockets on the front and leather patches on the elbows. I explained who I was and he immediately invited me in.

'You'll have to excuse the mess,' he said. 'We've been having a bit of work done. This is my wife, Gloria.' He introduced me to a small woman with brassy blonde curls. 'Glory, this is Sal. She's Daphne from downstairs's cousin. Thought she'd pop up and say hello.'

'That's nice. Put the kettle on then, dear. We'll all have a cup of Rosie.'

Her husband rolled his eyes. 'She means tea. Rosie Lea.'

'Oh, don't get all hoity-toity, Al.' Gloria looked at me and winked. 'He doesn't like me using slang in front of guests. Says it's common. Would you like to stay for supper, dear? Only we've got some nice crab paste. I'm going to make sandwiches.'

'Just tea thanks. I can't stay long.'

'Maybe another time, then. You and Daphne could both come. We've not had a chance to introduce ourselves properly since we moved in. It's all been a bit hectic.'

I looked around the flat. There were bare pipes running across the wall and disappearing down into the floor in one corner.

Gloria noticed me looking at them. 'It's a bit of a mess, isn't it? The plumbing was in a right state, so we've been having it redone. I'll be glad when it's all boxed in again and we can redecorate.'

I wondered why she was speaking so loudly. Maybe it showed on my face because she smiled apologetically and said in a more normal tone, 'Sorry, I get used to shouting. Al's a bit mutton. You know, Mutt and Jeff. Deaf.'

'Right.' Suddenly it was all beginning to make sense. 'So, all this is going to be boxed in again?'

'Yes. The builders will be back in on Monday. They've promised it will all be as good as new in a day or two.'

I spent another half hour chatting with Gloria and Al before I went back to Daphne's flat. On the way down the stairs I wondered what I should tell her. How can you disillusion someone that naïve? It would be like kicking a puppy.

In the end I went for a gentle letdown.

'I don't think Great Uncle Albert will be in touch

much more, Daphne. I reckon he just wanted you to know that he's fine.'

Surprisingly, she seemed quite relaxed about it. 'Well, if he does then I'm just happy that I've heard him, Sal. Besides, you never know. Now that I've started to channel these vibrations, who knows what I might pick up.'

What indeed? I hoped Al and Gloria's pipework was only exposed in their kitchen.

'You never know, Daphne. You never know.'

ABOUT 'THE PSYCHIC'

The paranormal world seems full of ruling bodies. From the White Council of Jim Butcher's *The Dresden Files* to the Ministry of Magic in the *Harry Potter* books and countless more besides, it seems there is always room for a group of know-it-all leaders to lay down rules and make life difficult for any independently minded protagonist. It felt only right that Sal and Daphne should have the threat of such an institution looking over their shoulders even if their outing in this story was just a bit of fun.

6

HOLD YOU LIKE A SPIDER

Nerys is wearing the blonde wig tonight. Ryan thinks of it as her work hair: neat and tidy but closer to mouse than many women would have chosen, designed to blend in rather than to attract attention. She has other wigs which are brighter and which he thinks suit her more, but he's pleased to see her whatever she has chosen to wear. She hasn't been in the Unicorn for over a week and he has missed her.

'Mind if I join you?' He stands by her table, drink in hand.

'It's a free country.' The slight pursing of her lips might have been a smile. 'Supposedly.'

Ryan hides a smile of his own. Caustic, opinionated and never afraid to share her views; that's Nerys – whatever her hair shade *du jour*. Some people might call her a character, and wouldn't mean it as a compliment, but her attitude is what Ryan likes most about her. She is interesting. There is no one else quite like Nerys.

'I didn't expect to see you here on your day off.'

'You almost didn't. I was feeling a bit rough earlier.' That earns him a hard stare. 'Don't worry, I'm not about to give you plague; it's hay fever. Usually, I'd suffer in silence, but Andy insisted on getting me some antihistamines.' He grins at the recollection. 'I took a couple earlier and I'm fine now.'

'Then why are you here rather than swanning around town with your boyfriend?'

'It's not like we're joined at the hip, Nerys. He's on call this week; we'll hook up again on Friday. Tonight, I wanted to check up on you.' Ryan thinks he has said the wrong thing as Nerys's expression hardens. For a moment it is like looking at a stranger. 'You've not been in for ages,' he explains, hurriedly. Then he adds a confession, 'I was worried.'

'Worried?' She seems taken aback by the idea. 'Well, you've no right to be.'

Ryan shrugs off the prickliness of her response

more amused than insulted. 'Like it or not some of us would miss you if you disappeared.'

A gravelly 'Speak for yourself' comes from the direction of the bar but, when Ryan turns to look at the landlord, Howell is studiously pulling a pint and doesn't meet his eye.

The image on the television screen above the bar catches Ryan's attention. Yellow and black police tape, strung between spindly trees, cordons off what looks like a drainage ditch somewhere in the middle of nowhere. In front of the tape a grim-faced reporter is delivering his piece to the camera. The sound is off but the subtitles across the bottom of the screen tell the story.

... ANOTHER BODY HAS BEEN FOUND ...

'That's why I was worried,' Ryan admits to Nerys, with a nod towards the television. 'He's killed another one.'

'Who has?'

'The Spiderman, of course.' At her blank look he adds, 'Oh, come on, Nerys. Some lunatic's killing delivery drivers and you're telling me you haven't noticed? It's been, what, five now?'

'Six.' Nerys's whisper is aimed down at her drink.

'Ah, so you have been following it.'

Nerys's scowl admits no such thing and Ryan chooses not to press the point although he is amused by her pretence of indifference. As the subtitles continue to scroll he says, 'Anyway, you're wrong. It says there that this was the fifth. Either way, it's too many.'

He expects Nerys to agree but instead she says, 'You'd think the press would have come up with something more original than the Spiderman.'

Ryan raises an eyebrow. Trust Nerys to express more offence over a detail like that than over the actual murders.

'What else are they going to call him when he wraps his victims up in duct tape? It's just like Spiderman and his spidey web.'

Nerys's mouth tightens in disapproval although Ryan isn't sure whether it is the lack of journalistic imagination or his own knowledge of superheroes that has earned her scorn.

'Well, I think it's stupid,' she says, 'bringing in some comic book reference. If they have to give the killer a name, why not just go with the Spider? Spiderman is insulting. It trivialises the whole business.' Her voice turns cynical as she adds, 'And that's another thing. I bet there wouldn't be half so much fuss if it was women getting killed. It would either be "They're all prostitutes," or "They shouldn't have been out on their own." But kill half a dozen men and that's a different story.'

Ryan doesn't know how to answer that. Rather

than try he says, 'The papers are saying the time between the murders is getting shorter. They reckon that's what happens with serial killers; they get used to the buzz and the need to kill builds up quicker each time they do it.'

'Oh, so now you're an expert on serial killers?'

'No. It's just what I read in the papers.' He looks down at his hands, suddenly shy. 'That's why I wanted to see if you were here tonight. You probably think I'm daft but with you doing more long haul work and then not coming in all week, I was worried.'

For a moment Nerys doesn't seem to know what to say. She turns the glass in front of her as though it were a compass and she was searching for north.

'I'm not sure whether to be flattered or insulted. I know I'm no model but are you saying I look like a bloke?'

'No, of course not.' Although she does – a little. Not that she's ugly but she has a plain, rather homely face which the short cut of her wig does little to enhance. Her figure doesn't help either. The cancer that had robbed Nerys of her hair had also taken her breasts. She hadn't bothered with reconstructive surgery – she told anyone who asked that she didn't see the point – so she has no curves. Her body is straight up and down and rather stocky if Ryan is brutally honest. 'It's just that in your work gear, in the dark, someone might ...' Ryan senses he is digging a hole for himself and stops. 'I was worried, that's all.'

Nerys mutters something which would make one of her fellow drivers blush and then sits in silence for a moment, considering.

'Tell you what, in future I'll make sure I wear my pink disco wig when I'm working at night.' She shakes her head. 'You don't need to worry. The boys at the depots look out for me, especially now. Besides, I've got no more long haul jobs scheduled for a while.'

She picks absently at her cuticles as she talks to him. They are raw and Ryan thinks that despite her bravado she is more concerned than she admits. He is about to suggest they talk about something more cheerful when he sees it on the wall behind her shoulder.

'Oh my God, there's a spider.' He can't help cringing.

Nerys looks at him, bemused. 'What's wrong with spiders?'

'Are you joking? All those legs. I hate them. They give me the creeps.' He shudders. 'Kill it.'

'Don't be stupid. Poor little thing's probably more scared of you.' To his horror she turns and carefully shepherds the monstrosity into her hand.

He shrinks away. 'How can you do that?'

'It's only a spider. Hang on a sec.'

Ryan watches incredulously as Nerys carries the

spider outside. He eyes her hands as she comes back to the table and she makes a point of showing him that they are empty.

'Better now?' Her tight-lipped scowl makes him feel like a toddler being reprimanded by an adult carer.

'You know the females eat the males after mating, right?'

'Yeah, and if it was the other way around no one would bat an eyelid. Let's have another drink. It's okay,' she adds as he starts to rise. Maybe this is her tacit peace offering. 'I'll get them.'

They sit for a while after that, talking and drinking. When Nerys looks at her watch and declares she needs to get going Ryan automatically stands with her. He is surprised when the world tilts sideways and his head spins.

'Are you okay? You're looking a bit green.'

'I think it's the antihistamines,' he groans. 'I probably shouldn't have had that second pint.'

'Blimey, you're a cheap date.' Nerys scowls. 'Hang on and I'll get Howell to call a taxi. You can wait for it out in the car park. You'll probably feel better in the fresh air.'

Nerys sits Ryan on the low wall separating the Unicorn's car park from the street. Although she had said she needed to go she seems to have decided to wait with him.

Still, she keeps checking her watch.

'Why isn't it here yet? It should be here soon.'

She sounds edgy, as though she is trying to reassure herself of that fact. Ryan isn't sure why but perhaps she wants to get rid of him before he is physically sick. The thought does nothing to ease his growing queasiness. Maybe he would be better waiting in the pub's toilet. He feels his stomach heave and lurches to his feet, just in time to throw up as the taxi pulls into the car park. Dimly he registers the squeal of tyres as the driver takes one look at the state of his would-be passenger, spins his vehicle around and drives off.

Nerys swears comprehensively and Ryan is surprised when she then turns on him.

'What did you do that for?' She seems unduly upset. 'He was meant to make sure you get home safely.'

Slowly Ryan straightens up. His stomach feels better now that it is empty, but his brain is fuzzy as though his head has been stuffed with cotton wool. All he wants is to go to sleep.

'You could take me home instead.' It seems the perfect solution.

'No.' Nerys's answer is sharp and emphatic. 'No, I couldn't.'

'Why not?' Ryan knows Nerys drives her own vehicle not a company one. ''S your van; your rules.'

'Because I don't want you in there. There are things I've got to do tonight. A job.'

She is agitated, breathing heavily, but then she composes herself. She jerks her head at the CCTV camera on the pub wall.

'Howell's going to rag you for puking in his car park.'

Ryan shakes his head and then wishes he hadn't as the world swings violently. 'No, he won't. The system's been down for ages. Don't tell anyone.' He raises a finger to his lips and then wags it in her face. 'There's no video at the moment.'

He can't understand why Nerys swears under her breath.

'I wish you hadn't told me that.' She hugs herself as though suddenly cold. 'I don't want this.'

'I won't be sick again. Honest. I'm just going to go to sleep.'

As if to demonstrate the truth of this Ryan makes a half-hearted attempt to lean on Nerys. She swears again but her words barely register as he misses her shoulder and crumples slowly to the ground.

Ryan isn't sure how long he has been asleep. He opens his eyes gradually and winces as he realises he is lying on cold metal. This must be the back of Nerys's van, he thinks and wonders why she was so fussy about having him as a passenger. It stinks like the pub toilets after a busy Friday night and of something else that he can't quite identify. There is a small light above him, sufficient to illuminate an untidy bundle shoved over to one side. That must be Nerys's next delivery, he decides. Whatever it is it can't be very valuable. It looks like nothing so much as a body rolled up in an old dust sheet. The thought amuses Ryan until he realises that the odd shape he can see sticking out of one end is the cleated sole of a work boot. That is the moment that he notices that his wrists are taped together and at the same time he understands what the other smell is. It is fear.

His head jerks round as he realises there is someone in the van with him.

'Nerys! What are you doing?' It is all he manages to say before she slaps a piece of duct tape over his mouth. His eyes widen as he sees what she is holding in her other hand. Carefully she smooths the tape down making sure it is secure and then she walks her fingers up his cheek. He is reminded of his mother playing Incy Wincy Spider with him as a child. He wants to vomit.

'I'm holding you,' Nerys says. 'Just like spider.'

ABOUT 'HOLD YOU LIKE A SPIDER'

This story sprang from the title – who would be holding you like a spider and what exactly would that mean? As for where the title came from, that's anyone's guess. In my first scribbled notes, Ryan's character was a young woman and my serial killer was male. Then I realised I was perpetuating the whole 'woman as victim' trope which, to my mind, has become an unhelpful cliché of the crime / thriller genre. Why shouldn't we have female serial killers bumping off men for a change?

7

SWANSONG

The first time we met was in a room crowded with people, dinning with noise and shoving bodies. You pushed your way into a space that wasn't really a space and I squished along to make room, ending up sitting with one cheek off the end of the bench to accommodate you. I took in your bright red hair and mirrored sunglasses.

'Hi. Are you registering for zoology too?'

I hadn't twigged that you were a mature student some nine years older than the rest of us. We must have seemed like children, irritatingly innocent and naive. You looked me over then turned away and I resolved to ignore someone so rude. And yet ...

And yet I kept noticing you, in lectures and in the labs, but I didn't engage. Then one day you spoke to me.

I was browsing the flea market in the Students' Union.

'This would suit you better.'

You held up a vivid purple shirt, thrusting it at me over the top of the beige cardigan I had been reaching for. I stood clutching it as you walked away. That shirt is still in the back of my wardrobe. Thinking about it makes me smile.

I was wearing it when I bumped into you and you introduced me to your companions.

'This is my friend Kim.'

Your friend? Really? How did that happen? And yet ...

Coffees grabbed between running for lectures. A shared room in a mid-Wales field centre, soaking wet and frozen but both fascinated by how fast a leech can move. The agonising intensity of finals. The euphoria of graduation. Stepping out into the world.

We moved to opposite ends of the country. Boyfriends became husbands. I married in Thailand. You married in the Witchfinder General's front room. We shared holidays: glaciers and desert sandstorms, Crusader castles ... running through the Siq to get back to the hotel for dinner having lost track of time searching for shards of Nabataean pottery and fat white scorpions in the ruins beyond the Treasury. Hastily washed hands and a spritz of perfume to cover the smell of dust ...

Yoga retreats and marathons became walking holidays that turned into walks in the garden and then seats in shaded corners when even walking became too much effort. The end came surprisingly quickly – a relief for us both, I think.

Now I'm waiting for you one last time. Behind me, the music starts and finally here you are. Not late, exactly – things couldn't start without you – but making an entrance, carried in by four strong men. As your sedan chair – no wheelchair for you! – passes you turn and smile as though you can see me still.

'Wouldn't miss this for the world,' I murmur, fingers stroking the Möbius loop we each had inked on our wrists on my 90th birthday, the tattooist unsure if we were crazy or cool. 'Best friends forever, remember.'

I grin as I fade away, leaving you to your 100th birthday party and your living friends.

ABOUT 'SWANSONG'

This was inspired by a prompt in *Writing Magazine* for short pieces on the theme 'Finding Friendship'. I decided to write about how I met my best friend at university. Some of it is true.

My friend and I are both still a fair way from the significant birthdays mentioned in the story so it remains to be seen how our personal ending will play out. However, on my last birthday I received a card from her stating, 'If I die first, I will haunt you'. This was before she had read the story, so who knows.

NB: for those of you who might be interested, one of the best ways to slow a leech down is to place it on a piece of tissue or kitchen paper.

8

SEEKING SHELTER

'So, you've seen it all now.' Rio's gesture took in the small apartment: the little kitchen off the open plan living area, the two bedrooms and the compact fresher unit between them. 'What do you think?'

Mia bit her lip. She liked it. Actually, she liked it a lot. The flat might be small but the floor-to-ceiling window in the main room allowed light to flood in. Mia could already picture Frankie's coloured glass mobiles hanging against it, filling the room with captive rainbows, her own hand-knotted rugs on the floor covering the worn places in the utilitarian carpeting. Of all the properties they had viewed, this was the nicest which was within their budget. But there was one major drawback.

'It doesn't have its own shelter.'

'Well, no. You can't expect a private facility for the money you'd be paying. There's a communal one in the basement, though. It's fully rated for the building size.'

Frankie tipped her head to one side and studied the site manager. 'I thought you said that's where the hydroponics are.'

Rio shrugged, his espresso-dark eyes rueful. 'It is.'

'Honestly? You've converted your fallout shelter into a hydroponics lab? I thought all buildings had to have a shelter.'

'Well, sure. Technically they do. But our community thinks that all of us having enough to eat is a better investment than preparing for some hypothetical future conflict that's probably never going to happen. It's all laid out in the paperwork, completely above board.'

He intercepted the frown Mia sent Frankie. 'Look, I understand if that's a showstopper for you. Some people worry more about what might happen tomorrow than what is happening today. That's not wrong, but it's not the way we roll. If things aren't right for you – well, no hard feelings. It's a shame though.' His expression was disarmingly open. 'I think you'd fit in, but it's got to be right for both sides.' He waited for a moment and then added, 'Just so's you know, we could refit the shelter in under two weeks and the building does have chem filters on all doors and windows. They kick in if the smog gets above a five.'

'Bio filters too?'

'You bet. Beta level.'

'Beta's not bad.'

There was a short silence and then Frankie said, 'The hydroponics lab: you said it's a communal facility?'

'Sure. The block committee meets regularly to decide what we're going to grow. We all get a say and we all get a share. D'you know much about hydroponics?'

'Frankie's an H1 technician.' Mia couldn't help the pride in her voice.

'An H1? Nice. You've got the smarts, kid. We've got an H3 who does our annual maintenance but an H1 ... I'll tell you what, if you do buy the flat I reckon the committee would give you extra credits if you'd be willing to put in time on the tanks. It's something to think about.'

'What made you do the conversion?'

'It was Kolya and Valentyna. They live in Flat 10. They had grandparents in Kyiv when ...' Rio's hands mimed a grisly parody of an explosion. 'You'd think if anyone was pro-shelter it'd be them, but no. "Feeding people today builds a peaceful tomorrow," they said and they kept saying it until they'd convinced everyone. Now we all benefit. Nice couple. They've got a toddler – a little boy. Cute as a button. This community's good for kids if you plan going down that route.'

'What do you reckon, love?' Frankie turned to Mia. 'I can imagine seeing you and Tiggy playing in front of that window when I come home from work.' She turned to Rio. 'Tiggy – Tegwen – is what we're going to call our daughter. When we have her.'

A smile spread across the site manager's face, bright as the sun burning through cloud. 'Seriously? You've got your approval?'

Frankie grinned. 'It came through last week.'

'Nice! Which one of you is going to carry? I mean, I'm guessing you can't afford the full *in vitro* business. You wouldn't be buying a flat here if you had that kind of money.'

'I am,' Mia said, shyly. 'But we wanted the natural option anyway.' Her hand slid to her belly as though she could feel the yet to come child growing there. 'And she's going to be Frankie's as well as mine. They'll take an egg from each of us to form her. That's how we know we'll definitely be having a daughter.'

'When the time comes,' added Frankie. 'We're on the list but it's going to be months yet.'

'And then the longest nine months ever.' Rio whistled and shook his head. 'That's nice, that really is.' He raised an eyebrow at Mia. 'Even more reason for you to be eating healthily, though.'

Mia looked around her. Everything about the flat was slightly shabby but in a way that felt homely rather than worn. It was like the balding ears of the old teddy bear she had loved into oblivion as a child. The extra food rations would be welcome but more importantly she wanted that sense of homeliness for herself and for Frankie and for Tegwen when their daughter was finally born. She caught Frankie's eye and nodded. Frankie broke into the widest of smiles.

'We're taking it.' She pulled Mia into a hug. 'Say hello to our new home.'

They moved in within a fortnight. The community in the flats was everything Rio had promised: welcoming and warm. They grew to know the other residents, becoming firm friends with Rio and his partner and picking up baby tips from Kolya and Valentyna while they waited for their own parenting journey to begin. Buying the flat was a decision neither of them regretted. At least not until the catastrophic day that the warning sirens sounded and all they could do was cling to each other and wait for the sun to be obscured in a flash of blinding white lig—

ABOUT 'SEEKING SHELTER'

The idea for this story came when I was running. I had started a writing course and the assignment prompt was to write a story where a house played a central role. I took a little liberty stretching the definition of a house to include an apartment, but I felt it worked.

Running brings out a nasty streak in me. The further I run, the worse predicaments and emotional turmoil my characters have to face. In the past I've stopped short of nuclear war, but I suppose there's a first time for everything. Perhaps I was having a particularly bad run.

The reference to Kyiv was prompted by the appalling situation in Ukraine and the war instigated by Russia. At the time I wrote the story the threat of nuclear weapons was being openly discussed.

9

FIRST BLOOD

In the moonlight the blood that ran down her body was black.

Amunet's foot caught against hard limestone. The fresh warmth on her skin told her she had cut herself but the thought seemed irrelevant. She took another step, stumbled – unable to help herself – fell, all her weight coming down on the edge of the step, on hip and rib. There was little enough breath left in her body but the pain drove it away. This time she wondered if it would come back. She wondered if she cared.

The remnants of her linen dress hung in shreds from her hips, nothing resembling the fine pleats which had graced her slender shape mere hours before. The rags that remained were soaked with blood and sweat and— no! She would not remember! Blood. Yes, let her remember the blood. Not all of that which clotted her body was her own.

Oh, but she had been proud of her body, delighting in the taut line of muscle over bone, the dark flash of her eyes and the raven-wing beauty of her hair, softer than corn-silk. She had been proud too that no man could have her, that she had chosen to give herself to the Goddess alone. Alas, that had turned out to be no more than a conceit. It had been a bitter lesson to learn that something she would never have given could instead be taken from her by force.

Fighting to stem the agony of anger and shame that flooded her mind in the wake of those memories, Amunet forced her head up and looked around her. What she saw had her recoiling in horror. How had she come here? She had no right – not now! – for around her Amunet recognised the plain limestone walls that marked the inner sanctum of the temple. While the outer courtyards might be painted in jewel tones, the walls adorned with prayers and with lists of sacrifices made, of battles won and of plunder donated to the temple, here there were no such distractions. There were no colossal statues designed to impress the worshippers with the might of their gods and the magnificence of their rulers. Here, where only the priestesses were allowed to enter, there was merely a small rectangular pool, positioned in the middle of the courtyard. Tiled in the same bone-white limestone as the courtyard walls and the steps that led up to it, nothing in the pool's appearance spoke of any great significance. Yet this was the true centre of the temple. Here, in its waters, was reflected the path of the moon – the Goddess in Splendour – as she travelled above the world each night.

Amunet sank back down onto the limestone tiles, her hand slipping forward to trail in the water. Blood ran down her fingers, spreading out in lazy tendrils, blooming like some alien riverweed. She should not be here. She was defiling the sanctum with her very presence. She, who had dedicated her life to serving the Goddess, had brought blood and dirt and filth to the heart of her worship. And to what end? Amunet knew no rite could purify her. She doubted she would even live until morning. Besides, she did not want purification. She wanted vengeance.

The thought gave her the strength to sit up. Addressing herself to the image of the Goddess in the water Amunet summoned the power that was hers – by birthright and training – and called upon the Mother. Pouring herself into a wordless, soundless plea she asked her Goddess to hear her. And suddenly She was there.

In the silent space between two heartbeats, where previously there had been only night, a woman stood. Slender as a papyrus column, her smooth, flawless skin shone like ivory through the fineness of the linen that wrapped her. Her blue-black hair was bound back with the Uraeus, the royal serpent of Egypt. A great pectoral of lapis and coral and gold spread from her shoulders to her breasts, its centre dominated by a winged scarab, while in her hands she held the crook and flail, the eternal symbols of rulership: the crook of the shepherd, tending the flock; the flail of the slave master, the one who must be obeyed.

'Mother, help me.' Amunet bowed her head, flattening herself to the ground before her Goddess.

'Do you ask for yourself, my daughter?' The voice was like the soughing of the wind across the desert, devoid of pity or feeling.

Yes, Amunet wanted to cry, but the word caught in her throat. 'No,' she said instead. 'I am beyond your pity. He who did this is no more. I have had my revenge, though I die for the taking of it.'

The Goddess seemed to look into the shadows for a moment. Not daring to turn her head still Amunet thought she saw a flash of sulphurous yellow eyes set in black skin above a long and pointed snout.

The Goddess nodded once and turned back to her

priestess. 'The balance holds,' she said. 'So, what else would you ask of me, oh my priestess who was?'

Amunet swallowed. 'There were others. They took Nephthys and ...' and here her voice failed her. The wall she had put between her and the pain crumbled like a child's mud dam against the Nile's flood and she wept, long racking sobs which tore at her throat. Something else tore inside her and she felt blood running again down her legs, could taste it, copper-sweet on her tongue. She pushed all thought of it away.

'... and Ta-amen.' The memory of the child nearly stopped her heart. 'She was my sister!' she cried. 'Her daughter was the child of my soul. They took them and then one by one they—'

'Hush.'

A cool hand touched her head, raising it so she could look into eyes darker than the night sky. As she did so the images in Amunet's mind faded. The colour drained from them until they were mere sepia tones, no longer the warm rose and cream of flesh nor the hot, violent blood-spatter of red. The pain shrank within her, not lessening exactly, but condensing into one small hard pebble under her heart. The edges of the pebble were smooth, like the rubbed surface of a touchstone.

'I would have revenge on those who did this. There is no one else. No one saw them. No one will stop them doing it again.'

'They will be judged when their time comes.' The Goddess's voice was serene, acknowledging the balance that lay at the centre of the universe. Of that balance Amunet had no doubt, but it was no longer enough for her to know that such a judgment followed inexorably on the heels of evil.

'But how many others will suffer before that time? How many other innocents?' It should have been inconceivable that she would dare to challenge the very Goddess she loved yet such was the strength of her emotion that Amunet did so without thought.

'It is true that innocents suffer.' The regal head did not dip but Amunet sensed the deity's acknowledgement. Then came her challenge. 'How else can it be when the strong do not help them?'

Amunet spoke from her heart without thought for the consequences. 'Let me help them. Let me be a tool of your vengeance.'

The world seemed to freeze into stillness in the wake of her words. There was no change in the Goddess's expression, but Amunet felt the terrible intensity of her gaze fall upon her.

'Do you know what you ask, child?'

Amunet forced herself to look up and into those night-dark eyes. Unblinking she held the Goddess's stare as she answered. 'Yes.'

Caught now, like a fly in amber, the wait for a response felt like an eternity.

'So be it.' The voice was merciless and final.

For a second Amunet quailed at the enormity of what she had done. Unable to undo her decision still she begged for some reassurance. 'Will I always be alone?'

The Mother looked down at her and her gaze was not without compassion. 'No. Not always. Others will come to you along the way, but the road will be hard, my daughter.'

Priestesses appeared as though conjured out of shadow. Perhaps they had been, for they were not the living women Amunet knew. Ivory-skinned and black-eyed as their mistress, they raised Amunet up, cutting the last remnants of her clothing from her with bronze knives. Two held her arms, supporting her, while a third poured water, from a large pitcher, over her head. The water washed away both the blood and the final traces of pain from her body before vanishing as though it had soaked into the limestone. Once she was clean they smoothed sweet smelling oil into her skin and then they dressed her again, binding back her hair with a fillet of gold.

Then the Goddess addressed her once more. 'This is my mark upon you.' Fingers, light as a kiss, touched

Amunet's brow. 'Only in moonlight will you go. The coin of men will be anathema to you. The metal it is made of will burn your skin. You cannot be bought: neither your vengeance, nor your mercy.'

As the Goddess spoke Amunet felt the power course through her. She felt herself changing, her senses becoming sharper, her body stronger, and yet she also felt the limitations the Goddess had placed upon her. In this, as in everything, there had to be balance.

'One final trial lies ahead of you, my daughter, before you can go forth. Answer with your heart and you will not fail.'

The Goddess seemed to grow in stature, her voice filling the temple. 'What is left when your friends are gone?'

Like an ancient liturgy the words rose in Amunet's mind. 'My strength.'

'What is left when your strength is gone?'

'My love.'

'What is left when your love is gone?'

'Hope.'

'What is left when hope is gone?'

'The Goddess.'

'What is left when the Goddess is gone?'

'It can never happen!' Amunet's body flooded with fear, denial, anger. Did the Goddess seek to trick her?

'What is left when the Goddess is gone?' Inexorable, undeniable, insistent, the voice came again, demanding that she answer.

And somehow, beneath the wrack of her emotions, Amunet found the strength to face a new and devastating truth. 'I am left when the Goddess is gone.'

There! She had said it. It was tantamount to blasphemy, but Amunet could now sense a time – so far off it seemed like an eternity away – when the worship of the Goddess would be forgotten. These temples, already so old, would be ancient then, buried and forgotten. Lost to the sands of the desert and to time itself. And yet, in that strange and distant world, she would continue. When her Goddess remained as only a memory in her heart, she would still be there, seeking through an eternity of nights to find those who preyed upon the innocents and to bring them face to face with justice.

'I am left when the Goddess is gone,' Amunet repeated, understanding the enormity of what she faced and accepting it as her fate. 'I am alone. I have only myself.'

'Is it enough?' the voice asked of her.

'It is enough,' she replied. And it was.

'It is done.'

The final words might have been only in her head. Amunet blinked. The temple around her was empty once more. She would have thought it all an illusion but there was no trace of her old clothing nor of the blood that had smeared the stones. Her body was strong and whole and, when she closed her eyes, she understood she could hear the lustful yearnings of the wicked. She could taste their dreams and through their dreams she would track them and bring them, one by one, to justice.

Amunet smiled, her lips drawing back over the perfect whiteness of her teeth. She drew herself to her feet and left the temple without a backward glance.

And so it was that the first vampire went forth to hunt.

ABOUT 'FIRST BLOOD'

'First Blood' is one of the earliest stories in this collection. Vampires were having something of a rebrand at the time of writing (the *Twilight* series comes to mind) and I started thinking about the origins of vampire kind.

The story's ancient Egyptian setting came from my imagination with no supporting research into sacred rites or patterns of worship. I apologise to any scholars of ancient Egyptian culture I might have offended as a result.

Though it could be read as such, the theme of this

story is not one of personal revenge. It is about the universe restoring itself to a state of balance. Balance is not the same as peace.

10

NEVER LEAVE

How do you threaten someone who's already dead? I suspect most people would consider the question ridiculous – and rightly so. Before moving into the Old Manse, I would have been one of them. I would never have credited that, within the month, I would find myself asking it in all seriousness.

Not that things had started out badly. It's true there was a slightly odd feel to the place when I moved in, something I hadn't noticed on my earlier viewing with the estate agent. More than once, as I unpacked, I found myself turning to see who was behind me, but of course there was never anyone there. Yet the sense of being scrutinised remained. Then there was the stretch of landing that always felt unusually cold and the odd soughing whisper I would hear late at night when the house was quiet. At first, I shrugged it off as a peculiarity of the ancient plumbing but, as the nights went by, I began to imagine I could hear words in that thin whisper of sound. It seemed as if someone was chanting, 'Never leave. Never leave,' over and over in a high, singsong voice.

Some people might have found such things disconcerting, but I pride myself on being level-headed. That and the fact that, following a somewhat messy divorce, what money I had left was tied up in buying the property. I had needed somewhere to live and the Old Manse had seemed like a bargain. Had I realised beforehand that my new home came with a resident ghost I might have declined to exchange contracts but afterwards I simply couldn't afford to up sticks and move elsewhere. Besides, I told myself, it wasn't much of a ghost. Cold spots on the landing and faint voices at night – so what? It was hardly the stuff of nightmares. It didn't occur to me to worry about it. Not at first.

Things changed when I knocked through the wall between the master bedroom and the box room beyond, to create space for an ensuite bathroom. It seemed my resident ghost didn't think much of the alterations.

Pictures I had hung the week before now refused to stay straight on the walls and doors started slamming shut for no apparent reason. Rooms would turn icy, and I began to catch glimpses of a figure at the top of the stairs. Faint and insubstantial, it would disappear as soon as I turned to look properly, but I had the impression that if I could just turn quickly enough, I would be able to make out a disapproving face. I never managed to, but it didn't stop me driving myself half mad trying.

I called the presence Emma after my ex – she had been a bit of a door slammer too and the name seemed to suit this latest one – but beyond that I did my best to ignore her. Perhaps she found my calculated indifference annoying, or maybe she took it as a challenge, either way the level of ghostly activity continued to build. More objects developed a tendency to move. At first it was smaller things: keys I had left in the kitchen would turn up in the lounge, apples from the fruit bowl would somehow see fit to relocate themselves to the bath. Gradually though, the items affected became larger. The storage jars on the kitchen shelves would rattle and shake alarmingly as I prepared my breakfast and on one morning I found my office chair halfway across my study. Still, I refused to be daunted. These ghostly pranks were irritating but it wasn't as though they caused actual harm and I resolved to carry on ignoring them. I can be stubborn when I want to be. Unfortunately, so could Emma.

Things came to a head the day after the en-suite was finished. I was vacuuming up the final traces of plaster dust, having hung two rather nice photographs – moody black and white beach scenes – on the wall, when the postman called. Leaving the cleaner running I dashed downstairs pointedly ignoring the cold spot on the landing as I did so. Yet, as I signed for my parcel, an odd sensation prickled the nape of my neck and I shuddered.

'Someone walk over your grave?' the postman asked.

I glanced behind me half expecting to see a shadowy form.

'Something like that,' I muttered and all but shut the door in his face in my hurry to get back upstairs. I didn't know what was going on but I was certain that Emma was up to something.

As I raced up the stairs it struck me that I could no longer hear the vacuum cleaner. When I reached the bedroom door I realised why. The cleaner was where I had left it, its power cable still snaking across the floor, but with one crucial difference: the entire length of the electric cord had been cut into neat, four-centimetre segments. I stared at it, not quite ready to believe what I was seeing, and as I stared my disbelief turned to anger. It wasn't so much the thought of having to buy a new vacuum cleaner that annoyed me as the sheer senselessness of this petty act of vandalism.

'This is it. This is the last straw!' I strode into the room, looking round for a target for my rage. The temperature plummeted but I took no notice. 'I've just about had it with you and your tricks. Moving bits and pieces around is one thing but you can't go around destroying stuff just because you feel like it.'

On the dressing table my screwdriver jerked and began to roll backwards and forwards as though pushed by an unseen hand. The sight only infuriated me more.

'This isn't your house.'

Movement seen from the corner of my eye had me whirling round. My coffee mug pirouetted on the windowsill, wobbled for a second and tipped over the edge. I lunged forward to catch it and got the dregs down my shirt for my pains. For a moment I stood there seething, coffee dripping from my fingers.

'You do realise you're dead, don't you?' I demanded.

There was silence. Then the bathroom door crashed back on its hinges hard enough to dent the new plaster. The box of screws rose from the floor and flew at my head. As I ducked something pushed past me, knocking me off balance, and running footsteps echoed across the landing. Moments later, from somewhere beyond the stairs, came the sound of broken sobbing.

'Fine!' I yelled. My heart was pounding but I was damned if I was going to be intimidated by a ghostly tantrum. Nor was I going to feel sorry for the author of those sobs. 'I'd finished in here anyway. I'm going out and you'd better have calmed down by the time I get back or I'll—' My words ran out mid-sentence. How do you threaten someone who's already dead? Then it came to me. 'Or I'll find myself an exorcist!'

I saw Emma properly for the first time that night. I was drifting off to sleep when an icy cold *something* brushed along my arm. Startled awake I sat up almost before I had opened my eyes. As I scanned the room, searching for what had woken me, I felt the mattress sink slightly as someone sat down on the end of the bed ... and there she was.

Pale as a cobweb in the bright spill of moonlight, I could make out every detail of her face from her snub nose to her dainty, pointed chin. She was far younger than I had imagined. I had thought I was dealing with an adult but the apparition gazing at me was that of a child of maybe eight or nine. She wore a plain, dark dress which came down to her knees and woollen tights of a similar shade with flat, lace-up boots on her feet. Her long, straight hair was tied back with ribbons and in one hand she clutched a doll with a porcelain face. As I stared at her she looked back at me with eyes I somehow knew had been the colour of cornflowers.

'Hello Emma.'

Incredibly, my heartbeat which had been racing from my sudden awakening began to settle and I realised that, contrary to any logic, I wasn't afraid. I couldn't bring myself to feel anything but pity for this lost child.

'Was this your home?'

Her expression didn't change but I thought I felt a sense of agreement.

'I guess you didn't like me knocking that wall down, huh?' The bottom lip of her rosebud mouth stuck out in a pout so typical of a young child that I had to hide a smile. 'I'm sorry about that. You do know you shouldn't be here though, don't you?'

Emma's grip tightened on the doll as she brought it across her lap. I felt mean, as though I was about to break it to her that there was no Santa Claus, but I knew this was something she had to be told. I tried to make my voice gentle, but firm.

'You should have moved on,' I explained. 'When you ...'

I hesitated, unable to bring myself to say *when you died*. Instead, I tried to recall exactly what my friend Harry had told me when I'd phoned him that afternoon. Harry and I had shared a flat together at university. He's a spiritualist: a little kooky in his beliefs but he had always taken my ribbing in good humour and was generous enough not to throw it back in my face when I explained my current predicament. Holding to his advice I tried again.

'When it was time for you to leave this life there was another place for you to go to.'

On the end of the bed Emma rocked the doll in her arms. Not looking up at me she shook her head. 'Never leave. Never leave.' She rocked the doll in time with the words: the same singsong chant I had heard before. I felt a vague sense of unease at the conviction carried in that childish voice.

'Why Emma? Why can't you leave?'

But she faded away, leaving me wondering what puzzle I had unearthed.

It took me a couple of days to arrange things – retirees have fuller diaries than you might expect – but Thursday morning saw me meeting with the head of the local history society. Over a pot of tea in Dolly's Corner Café, Rose Trecarrell regaled me with the sad story. In 1913 the manse had been home to a minister, Edward Munroe, his wife Rachel and their young daughter, Emma. I got goosebumps when Rose told me the name, and yet I wasn't surprised. Whether by coincidence or influence, now I knew why it had struck me as being so appropriate.

By all accounts the couple were well-liked, and they doted on their only child. Life seemed good for the Munroes but that summer Emma was taken ill with a devastating fever. The doctor was summoned but, as Rose told me, with a degree of relish that only the old can put on death, 'He took one look at the child and pronounced there was nothing he could do. "She would never leave her bed," he said.'

Sadly, it was as the doctor predicted. Emma died shortly afterwards.

I found the graves just behind the village church in a quiet spot which Rose had described to me. Edward and Rachel Munroe lay together, their tombstone almost hidden beneath the spreading branches of an ancient yew. Alongside them was a second, smaller stone, its inscription barely legible after more than a century of weathering: Emma Munroe. I sat there for some time thinking over what Rose had told me. Then I went home and phoned Harry.

I waited for sunset before lighting the candles. I wished Harry could have made the trip from Birmingham to join me but he was busy and I felt a responsibility to Emma to try and resolve things as soon as possible. So, instead of Harry's reassuring presence, I had a sheet of hastily scribbled instructions – a sort of idiot's guide to holding your own séance. I hoped it would do.

Also on the floor in front of me, carefully arranged on layers of protective tissue, were two items from the history society's archives. The first was a rather natty looking Bowler hat – something I had only ever associated with city gents and 1970s TV secret agents, until Rose put me straight on their broader appeal in late Edwardian Britain. The second was a lady's evening fan. Both had belonged to the Munroes and Rose had mentioned having them during our first conversation. I had coaxed and browbeaten her into lending them to me after my phone call with Harry. While it wasn't strictly necessary to have such personal effects, he had said they would help a beginner like me form the necessary connection. I wasn't proud: I wanted all the help I could get.

Wondering what I was letting myself in for I placed my fingertips against the hat's black felt brim and the cool ivory blades of the folded fan. I had had to promise Rose I wouldn't over-handle them, but she had said it was okay to touch. I sent her a silent thank you and then began reading the words Harry had given me, focussing on what I wanted to happen.

My mystic friend hadn't said how long the process might take but nothing seemed to be happening. Time passed and my knees started to twinge from sitting cross-legged while my head throbbed with the effort of concentrating. It was no use, I decided. I'd given it my best shot, but nothing was going to happen. What had I expected? I'd phone Harry in the morning and make arrangements for him to visit. Maybe he would have more luck. But, as I moved to uncross my aching legs, the atmosphere in the room changed.

It wasn't the drop in temperature that signalled Emma's presence. This was a movement of air as though a door had opened and through it came a soft breeze, scented like a summer meadow. The figures of a slightly built man and an equally slender woman appeared just beyond my circle of candles. My throat constricted and all the hairs stood up on the back of my neck as I looked at them. My heart was hammering against my ribs, not so much in fear but in wonder at what I was seeing. Even after my encounter with Emma it hardly seemed possible.

Scarcely daring to breathe I waited for what I hoped would happen next. Time seemed to hang and then, sweeter than anything I had seen before or since, the shape of a young girl materialised between the two apparitions.

The man looked at me and inclined his head in a politely formal nod of acknowledgement, but he was smiling as he did so and the woman mouthed the words, 'Bless you,' her own face lighting with pleasure. As for the little girl, well she waved before she took her parents' hands. I desperately wanted to speak to them, to say something, to wish them well, but no words came. For a moment longer the three figures lingered and then, between one heartbeat and the next, they were gone.

That night the Old Manse was quiet for the first time since I had moved in. There were no voices to be heard, just the creaking of an old building settling into its beams. Nothing moved from its accustomed place and for once I didn't find myself shivering as I crossed the landing. Everything was as it should be and a sense of peace lay over the house. And that is how it has remained to this day. Over the years I have often thought of Emma but I have neither seen nor heard her since that night. It seems she finally managed to leave.

ABOUT 'NEVER LEAVE'

A gentle ghost story. Not all spirits are terrifying or vengeful and it is possible to encounter paranormal activity with a sense of surprise and wonder rather than fear.

Something similar to the vacuum cleaner incident was related to me by a family friend. They put it down to a previous resident taking against their attempt to clean up a long-disused cellar. I can't recall if they found an alternative way to finish their cleaning (personally, I'm all for reasons not to take on more housework!) but I do remember their main emotion being one of annoyance at the destruction coupled with amazement at how the power cable remained in position, albeit in two-inch chunks – a detail that I've updated from Imperial to Metric in my story.

11

THE GLASS SLIPPER

'She did what?' Claudia stared at her sister in disbelief.

'I'm telling you, she left one of her shoes behind.' Nicole dropped down into the chair opposite, in a flounce of tiered skirts, and put her head in her hands. 'I can't believe it!' she moaned. She raised her head a little, meeting her sister's eyes. 'The Godmother's going to kill her.'

'The Godmother's going to kill us more like it. You know Cindy's her favourite. I tried telling her that the girl wasn't ready to go on a job yet, but she wouldn't listen.'

Nicole nodded sadly. 'It wasn't as though she had

to do anything difficult. All she had to do was distract the Prince while we got into the royal bed chamber.'

'Well, she certainly managed that part of the job alright. Although, from the way she was talking when she got home, I'm surprised we didn't bump into her in the royal bed chamber. *The Prince said this, the Prince said that.*'

'*The Prince had his royal hand on my bum all evening.* I know. I couldn't believe the way he was all over her on the dance floor. And she just let him!'

'No class, no finesse.'

'No, but you have to agree she's good with her hands.'

'The Prince would certainly agree. Did you see what she was doing with his codpiece?' Claudia fanned her face. 'Goodness, the youth of today. I'm blushing just thinking about it.'

'All in the name of getting the job done, or so she said, but you could see she was enjoying it. And it was all over the papers this morning. Mystery woman leaves Prince standing at masked ball.'

The two sisters eyed each other. Media attention was not something they courted.

'Thank goodness she made it back to the getaway coach on time,' Nicole said, trying to find something positive in the night's work.

'Only just. Twelfth stroke of midnight is cutting

things a little too fine if you ask me. And then she blows it all by leaving traceable evidence behind. Hasn't she learned anything we've been trying to teach her?'

'Buttons won't have had time to fence the jewels yet. All those diamonds: not even the Godmother could make those disappear overnight.'

'You know Sergeant Dandini will have his forensics team busting a gut to trace that shoe.'

'It won't be easy. The Godmother had them handmade.'

'True, but I'll bet there's enough dirt on the sole for them to run a soil analysis and get a good idea of where it's been worn. Plus, Cindy was taking it on and off, on and off, so she could admire it. She must have left her prints all over it.'

'Magic glass, remember? It shouldn't hold prints.'

'Well, I hope for everyone's sake it doesn't.'

'Okay, let's look at this logically. They have the slipper but that's all. The coach was at the breaker's yard within the hour, the coachman and grooms have got new jobs and the horses will have had their coats dyed, their shoes changed and be halfway to a stud farm somewhere across the kingdom border by now.'

'They'll be taking a one-way trip to the dog food factory more like it. And that's where we'll be going if we don't sort this. The Godmother will blame us. You know she will.'

'But what could we have done? The coach had to be out of there by midnight so we could make the drop-off. It's not like we could have gone back.'

'She'll still blame us.'

The two sisters lapsed into gloomy silence. They both knew it was true.

Eventually, Claudia stirred. 'What annoys me is how little respect we get. No one acknowledges the hours we spend planning these heists.'

'And all Cindy can do is keep moaning about us sleeping in late and making her do all the housework. If she was out all night casing joints and meeting fences then she'd know how much work goes into these fun little jaunts she's so anxious to get involved in.'

'You're right. And as for all the complaints about not having fancy clothes to wear. Does she think we enjoy being dressed up like this? I mean, look at me. There are all those lovely shift dresses this season but I end up with all these flounces. I look like one of the Palace Guards in drag.'

'Strong is beautiful,' Nicole reminded her. 'Whereas I look like a floor mop wearing a wig.'

'Don't be silly, darling; you're willowy. That's why you're such a good cat burglar.'

'Thank you, Claudie. But just once it would be

nice not to have to look ridiculous so people don't take us seriously.'

'I'd settle for a conversation where I didn't have to prattle on about marrying Prince Charming. You realise we're going to have to cover for her?'

'What do you mean?'

'Assuming they trace the shoe here – and we have to work on the principle that they will – we're going to have to pretend it belongs to one of us. How tight is your alibi?'

'Watertight. My—'

Nicole's answer was cut short by a loud knocking, coming from the front door, followed by the muffled sound of voices. Moments later the family steward appeared at the entrance to the parlour.

'Sergeant Dandini and several members of the Palace Guard request an audience, my ladies. I tried to dissuade him, but the sergeant was most insistent that he see you. I took the liberty of showing him and his men into the front salon.'

'Thank you, Randolph. We'll be along shortly.'

The steward bowed and retreated. Claudia and Nicole exchanged horrified glances.

'They can't have traced the slipper here that quickly, surely?'

'They must have. It's either that or someone's

grassed on us.'

'Who would do that? The Godmother would turn them into a frog.'

'It doesn't matter. We'll just have to deal with it. Oh, if we don't get arrested I'll have that girl sweeping out grates for a month! You go up to her room and tell her to stay there. Lock her in if needs be, we daren't let her speak to them. Then come and join me in the salon.'

'Why Sergeant, how lovely to see you.' Claudia simpered and fluttered her false eyelashes outrageously as she moved in to plant a kiss on her visitor's cheek. Dandini sidestepped her advance with an ease born of long practice.

'I'm here on official business, madam.'

'Of course you are.' Claudia swatted him lightly on the arm with her fan. 'And you've brought some of your men too. You Palace Guards are so devilishly handsome. It's enough to get me all hot and flustered.' She raised her fan to her face and then peeked at him, coyly, over the top.

Dandini met her gaze coolly. 'I need to talk to you about an item that was recovered from the Palace, yesterday evening.' The sergeant gestured and one of the guards stepped forward, holding out a plastic evidence bag. The missing glass slipper glistened inside it, sparkling like a handful of diamonds. 'Do you recognise—'

'Oh, you've found my shoe! You sweet man! Aren't you wonderful.' Claudia flung out her arms and engulfed the sergeant in a hug.

He struggled free with as much dignity as he could muster. 'Really madam.' He straightened his tunic. 'Am I to take it that you admit that this item is yours?'

'Well of course it is. Who else would it belong to?'

'It doesn't appear to be your size.' Dandini looked pointedly at Claudia's feet.

Claudia wilted a little under his gaze. Her lower lip trembled, fractionally. 'That's an extremely hurtful thing to say, Sergeant.'

Unrepentant, Dandini stared at her. 'So why should I believe that this is your shoe?'

'Because it is! Oh alright, I admit it; they don't fit terribly well.' Claudia treated Dandini and his men to a moue of disapproval as if she had been forced to confess to something distasteful. 'But I saw them when they were in the sales – do you have any idea how much glass slippers cost, Sergeant Dandini? – and I had to have them for the ball, to go with my new gown. I knew they weren't my size but sometimes a lady has to suffer for her beauty.' She gave the men a tremulous smile. 'That's why I changed my shoes just before I left the ball. I simply had to; my poor feet were killing me and I didn't think anyone would notice. When I got home and realised I must have dropped one I was mortified. But I should have known you'd come to my rescue.'

She fluttered her fan artfully and was reaching for the evidence bag as the salon door burst open.

'That's my slipper!'

Claudia looked round in horror at the new arrival. 'Really, Cindy dear—'

A breathless and slightly dishevelled Nicole appeared in the doorway behind her younger sister. 'Oh, Sergeant Dandini, what a nice surprise,' she said, treating him to a glowing smile as she edged over to Claudia. 'I couldn't stop her!' she breathed.

'I said, that's my slipper.' Cindy stood in the middle of the room, her hands on her hips.

'Cindy, don't be silly, darling. You know that's not true. She has such a vivid imagination, Sergeant, and I'm afraid to say that she's always coveting my clothes.'

'You weren't even at the ball, Cindy. Don't you remember? We wouldn't let you go. You told all your friends on social media how mean we were. You should read some of the things she posted, Sergeant. I don't like to use the word ungrateful, but …'

'I was at the ball. That is my slipper and I can prove it.'

'Cindy—'

The sergeant cleared his throat. 'I'm sorry ladies.' He sounded anything but. 'I'm going to have to take you all in for questioning in relation to a serious crime that took place at the Palace last night.'

There were two coaches waiting on the drive. As the Palace Guards ushered Claudia and Nicole towards the first one, Dandini held Cindy back.

'Not you. You're travelling separately.'

Shocked, Claudia twisted round in the grip of her burly escort. 'Don't worry Cindy,' she sought to reassure the younger woman. 'There's obviously been a terrible mistake, but we'll get things sorted out. Don't be frightened, darling and don't answer any of their questions before—' Her words were cut off as she was bundled unceremoniously into the coach and the door slammed shut behind her.

Dandini escorted Cindy over to the second vehicle. It bore the insignia of the Palace Guard but closer inspection showed it to be more sumptuously decorated than the first.

'She's all yours, Your Highness.' Sergeant Dandini handed Cindy up to the man sitting inside.

There was a brief silence as the coach's occupant gazed at her. 'You did it, Cindy! Oh, I've been so scared in case anything went wrong and they suspected you.'

The Prince kissed Cindy's hand but, when he tried to move the kiss up to her lips, she pulled away, evading his display of affection.

'Oh no you don't, Charming,' she said, giving him a knowing smile. 'You're not getting your hands on my crown jewels until I see that royal pardon we agreed on.'

ABOUT 'THE GLASS SLIPPER'

This story first appeared in the anthology *The Forgotten and the Fantastical 5,* published by Mother's Milk Books Ltd. I can't recall why the dark recesses of my mind threw up the idea of the Fairy Godmother as the head of a crime syndicate but from there it was no great leap to having the glass slipper as a piece of evidence in a criminal investigation. And that was as far as it went. Like many of my writing ideas it got parked, awaiting that semi-mythical future day when I would have 'time' to work on the story properly. I jotted down a few notes to remind myself of my idea and then forgot about it.

Fast forward several months and I found myself at FantasyCon, listening to a panel session on myths and fairy tales. Talking to Teika Bellamy at the Mother's Milk stand afterwards, she told me about the anthology. I mentioned my take on Cinderella and she suggested I should buy a book and submit the story. A clever sales pitch perhaps, but fortunately it came with the happy ending of her liking the story enough to include it in the anthology. However, that moment was still in the future. At the time I spoke to Teika, I hadn't yet written the story, but here was my incentive to do so. As in all good fairy tales it was completed – if not on the stroke of midnight – certainly on the afternoon of the 30th November deadline.

12

SKIN DEEP

'It's alright for you.' Jennifer's cocktail glass tipped dangerously as she gestured with one manicured hand. 'You'll go home, have zero sleep and look just fine in the morning.' She aimed a mock scowl at her best friend. 'The rest of us will be slumped at our desks looking like death warmed over. It is so not fair.' She pouted and took another sip of the pink concoction in her glass.

'I'm pulling a duvet day,' Lauren declared. 'Can't party like we used to, eh girls?'

There were nods all round.

'It's one of the downsides of getting older,' Suzie

agreed.

'Not that you look it, Birthday Girl. You don't look a day over ...' Jennifer squinted theatrically. 'Forty-nine. Definitely nowhere near the big five-oh.'

'Not even near the big four-oh,' Lauren sighed. 'I wish I had skin like yours, Suz. You're going to have to let us in on your secret one day.'

'It's not down to me. I have my grandmother's skin. I inherited it from Mum.' Suzie sipped her own cocktail. 'You have to choose your parents wisely.'

'To be fair, your mum did have amazing skin. No one would have guessed how old she was.'

'Granny's skin. I was lucky she passed it on to me.'

'You didn't always have good skin though,' Jennifer noted. 'I remember you as a teen. Spotty Dotty, we called you. Remember that?'

'Don't remind me!' Suzie had spent years living that down. 'Luckily we're late bloomers in my family.' She patted her cheeks. 'So, who's for another drink?'

Later, as she took off her makeup, Suzie checked her reflection in the bedroom mirror.

Not bad.

Although there were dark circles showing under her eyes. It was getting harder to party until the wee hours. Come midnight, all her friends had been ready to go home. 'Before we turn into pumpkins – with skin to match,' Jennifer had said. Suzie smiled. She had a remedy for that.

Bending down, she withdrew the old vanity case she kept under her dressing table. The exterior was faded and cracked, but it was what was inside that was important. She flipped the clasps and reverently withdrew the tightly wrapped bundle from within. The familiar smell of cold cream and an odd, sweet perfume washed over her as she unrolled the headscarf-sized sheet of what appeared to be fine chamois leather.

Suzie settled under her duvet, carefully smoothing the leather over her face, pressing it against her features. The sheet was getting more brittle now. She supposed it was inevitable – she and Mum had lived and partied hard. Maybe it was fortunate she didn't have a daughter of her own to leave it to. Still, hopefully it was good for a few more decades.

She looked out through the eye holes as she turned to switch off her bedside lamp.

'Night night, Granny,' she murmured, feeling the warm tingle of the magic starting to work. Smiling, Suzie lay back and let her grandmother's skin do its job.

ABOUT 'SKIN DEEP'

My mum has beautiful skin and looks far younger than her chronological age. When we talk about it, she says it's because she inherited her mother's skin. I know she is referring to genetics but I couldn't help playing with the idea of this being a literal statement.

13

NIGHTSHADE

There are many stories that have sprung up around the woman they call Bella Donna. She is impossibly old. She is incredibly young. She is beautiful, ugly – invisible even! She does not exist; she is only a myth. But those who say that cross themselves or make the sign against evil even as they speak, for we know in our hearts she exists. Death exists for everyone.

Her notoriety is such that even those outside the shadowy world of the trade have heard of her. They call her the assassin's assassin, as though that were an honour we had bestowed upon her: recognition that she is the best of us. The truth is simpler. She is the assassin of assassins:

the killer skilled enough to kill other killers.

Legend says she is as remorseless as the north wind, that she will track her target across miles and years until they have tried and exhausted every avenue of escape, until they no longer have the heart to run. Only then, when they have given up in all but name, will she reveal herself. They say she is seen by no one who is not ready to die.

I do not know why my mind has turned to her this evening. Perhaps it is because I am old. Not many of us get to achieve such a thing, but I have. It is a victory of sorts but one that comes with its own price. My right leg aches where a bullet fragment remains lodged against the bone. It happened a long time ago. I can no longer run and, in the cold, I limp and yet I am still here.

I walk slowly through the narrow streets beyond the old Jewish cemetery. The dusk is thickening towards full dark and the air is growing chill. Already I feel my leg stiffening.

'Are you lost, Grandad? Need someone to help you find your hotel?'

The voice startles me from my reverie and I curse silently. In truth, it seemed that I had been aware of the footfalls tracking me for some minutes and yet I had paid them no heed. My usually sharp sense of self-preservation had not kicked in. It does so now.

'No, that won't be necessary, thank you.' I speak confidently, as though the offer of help is genuine, and draw myself up to my full – if unexceptional – height. I know I am small and my appearance is unassuming. That is why I have been so successful: I do not look dangerous. It is that which has put me in danger now.

The young men laugh. There are two of them, thick-set and muscular, filled with the arrogance of youth.

'I don't think you understand, Grandad.' The speaker steps closer while his companion moves sideways to block me, should I try to flee. 'It's not an offer you can turn down. But play nice and give us your wallet and we'll point you back to the right side of town.'

'And if I don't?'

The question seems to confuse him; perhaps no one had asked him this before. For a moment he doesn't know what to say. Then his expression darkens.

'If you don't, we'll take your wallet anyway and I'll take the price for doing so out on your hide. You'll be sleeping in an alley tonight, Grandad, and I don't think you'll be waking up again.'

He takes another step. There is no hurry; in his mind his prey is cornered and defenceless.

'I see.' Stupidity is not a crime in most countries. In my world it is a capital offence. And yet, I do not want to kill him. I give him one last chance. 'You are much younger than me. You are heavier and stronger, taller which gives you more reach in a fight.' All this is true. Anyone judging us would say that the odds are stacked heavily in my aggressor's favour. 'So, perhaps you should ask yourself why it is that I am not frightened of you.'

I wait for him to process what I have told him, both the spoken and unspoken messages. He does so, but he does not reach the conclusion I had hoped.

'I think it's because you're simple, old man!'

He lunges on the last word, meaning to grab me, but I have seen his muscles tense and anticipate the move. I may be unable to run but I am faster than he expects. Not for nothing did my first teacher call me Koshka – the cat. I pivot on the balls of my feet, my left hand sweeping across my body to guide his reaching hand past me. His momentum carries him forward. Had I not moved he would have crashed into me like a juggernaut of human flesh. Now his charge works against him as I drive my right hand out, the thumb folded in against the palm, the fingers locked together to create a rigid blade of muscle and bone, that connects with the soft flesh of his throat.

There is a perfect second when all motion seems to cease and the world is silent.

Then my attacker drops to the ground, clawing at his throat, flailing and thrashing. He cannot cry out for his larynx is crushed. Nor can he breathe.

His eyes are wide and white, rolling with fear. In his affliction he has forgotten all about me. He will be unconscious in less than a minute and dead in little more than three. Nothing short of an emergency tracheotomy will save him now and, even if I could render him such help, still I would choose not to. His recklessness has killed him. Yet I feel no satisfaction, no pleasure in that truth.

His companion stares in horror at his fallen comrade and then at me. I read anger on his face and also fear and wonder which he will listen to.

'You cannot help him.' I tell him this because it is true, hoping it will help him make the right choice. 'You should leave here, now.'

His face contorts into a snarl and I understand that he has chosen to listen to his anger. It is not what I had hoped for. Until this evening I had not killed in years. Doing so again gives me no pleasure but I would rather that than die at the hands of a fool. When he pulls a knife from beneath his jacket I know the choice has been made for me. The blade shows a dull silver in the fading light and he slashes it in front of him as though gutting an invisible deer. He means to unman me, to cow me with his prowess and I sigh, saddened by his display but unafraid. If anything, I feel wearied by his bravado as I slip my own knife from my sleeve and we face each other.

At least he has learned from his friend's fate,

enough not to commit himself to the first stroke. He feints and I give ground, respecting the blade if not the man who wields it. Like his friend he is taller than I am and that gives him the advantage. To strike him I will have to step within his reach and, while he wields a knife, that could be fatal. But I cannot delay for too long. He has not thought of it yet, but he has the stamina to wear me down with this deadly dance. If he realises this I am dead, for I cannot run away.

The next time he feints I sidestep, but he anticipates my move and follows, closer than I had expected. My foot catches on the cobbles as I turn and suddenly he is inside my guard, a feral cry sounding in his throat as he sees his opening and stabs towards my gut. It is my bad leg that saves me. As I twist violently to avoid his blade it gives beneath me and I fall sideways. I would not have gone to the ground deliberately – a man on the floor in a fight is a dead man – but as I fall I roll, not away from him, where he might come at me as I rise, but almost under his feet. He is hampered by my closeness and I risk him slicing the arm I throw up as a block even as I make my own attack, striking up, my knife finding the femoral artery. His death is messier than his friend's but quicker.

I regain my feet slowly. The night smells sickeningly of the waste my attackers' bodies have voided as they died and of the blood which covers me. I realise then that some of it is my own. My opponent's knife has caught me after all. I put my hand to my side. The wound hurts, but not with the red, bubbling, fighting-for-breath hurt of a compromised lung. I do not think it overly serious, but it will need stitching. I can do that. I know where to get the necessary equipment, the painkillers, the antibiotics. But I will have to go to ground. I press my palm against my wound to staunch the flow of blood and, for a moment, I feel sick at the thought and tired, so very tired.

'Why couldn't you have left me alone?' I cry to the encroaching night. All I had wanted was to be left in peace. I have grown tired of running, of the fight to stay unrecognised and unnoticed in a world of increased surveillance.

And that is when I hear it: my name whispered breathy and low and sweet as a half-remembered love song.

'Pietr.'

This is the first time in many years that I have heard it spoken, its syllables rich with the accent of the northern forests and warm as the white nights of summer. I have no friends to call me by it and I know that it is her.

There is no fear, no spiky blood-rush of adrenalin. I stand and listen for a moment and a sense of peace steals over me. I realise I am ready. With her name on my lips I turn to face the last person I will ever see.

ABOUT 'NIGHTSHADE'

One of my favourite short stories is 'Shadder', by Neil Gaiman. You can find it in his anthology, *Trigger Warning,* if you're not familiar with it. On the surface, 'Nightshade' has little in common with 'Shadder' but the idea of an inexorable, indefatigable hunter must have lodged in my brain and the concept re-emerged in this short story. Like the Shadders in their story, the eponymous Nightshade doesn't appear. She simply lurks in the background, waiting to make her presence felt at the very end.

14

THE REMNANT CHILD

Gwyn wasn't looking for trouble that afternoon. If she had had the slightest inkling of what was to come, she would never have chosen that particular route, or at least she would have waited until both she and the wizard were fully recovered before doing so. Their recent encounter with the Unseen Realm had brought them too close to death for comfort. If indeed it was ever possible to become comfortable with such a thing. Gwyn wasn't sure that it was – not for her, at any rate. She chose not to dwell on whether the same was true for Marcus Eldritch. Either way, all she wanted was a quiet walk in the late afternoon sunshine: sufficient gentle exercise to help two recuperating bodies back towards health with the added benefit of building an appetite for dinner. What could possibly go wrong?

Automatically turning up the footpath that wound away from the river, Gwyn was several yards along it before she registered the fact that Eldritch had not followed her. She turned back, momentarily concerned that something was wrong, and saw he was contemplating the old wooden footbridge, just visible through the stands of hawthorn and ash.

'What? What is it?'

The wizard didn't answer. Instead, he bent to pick something from the long grass. As he straightened Gwyn eyed him and his prize quizzically. Clutched in his left hand – for his right was encased from knuckles to elbow in a plaster cast – were two pieces of hawthorn twig.

Eldritch's lips quirked when he saw her expression. He had a wolfish smile, one which he used to good effect to mask his true feelings, but the grin he offered her now was genuine, transforming his rather saturnine face and wiping years from it.

'Surely the ancient art of Pooh Sticks hasn't completely missed Wales?' he asked, offering her the choice of the two sticks he held.

Gwyn couldn't help but laugh in return. 'Marcus

Eldritch, you're a fraud,' she proclaimed with a disbelieving shake of her head as she walked back to rejoin him. 'You go around masquerading as this all-powerful wizard and yet here you are challenging me to a child's game.'

'Pooh Sticks is a fine literary tradition,' Eldritch countered.

'Hmm ...' But despite her disparaging tone Gwyn's eyes twinkled and she gave the two pieces of wood the careful consideration of one choosing a rapier for a duel. 'This one,' she declared and grabbed it from the wizard's hand as though he might deny her her choice.

Eldritch's eyebrows raised at her fervour but all he said was, 'Are you absolutely sure about that?'

In response Gwyn ducked past him and all but ran for the bridge. 'Come on then. On the count of three.'

As the sticks dropped Gwyn hurried to the downstream side of the bridge, ready to judge the winner. Her eyes narrowed when she saw whose it was. 'You cheated. You hexed my stick.'

'I did not.'

'Huh! I should know better than to play games with a wizard.' She scowled and tossed her hair back: a theatrical gesture designed to show she was teasing. Mostly.

'As if you don't have more than enough power of

your own. Gwyn ...'

Rare as it was, Eldritch's use of her name silenced Gwyn's automatic protest. The Englishman leaned against the wooden handrail beside her, arms folded, his broken wrist in its rather grubby plaster cast cushioned on his left forearm. For a moment neither spoke, watching the tumbling brown water below them. The river wasn't overly deep but after the recent rains it was flowing fiercely.

'You told me what happened, but that was – what? – twenty-five years ago? You burned out your energy channels. Well, play unprotected with that much wild magic and I'd be amazed if you hadn't.' Eldritch's voice softened as he turned to look at her. 'I know what it's like to handle that stuff. I wouldn't dare do that unprepared. But you did and you survived.'

'Survived to know that I'd cauterised every energy path in my body,' Gwyn retorted, yet her tone was less venomous than her words. Not so long ago she would have taken Eldritch's comments as a judgement and met them accordingly – with defiance. Now she wasn't quite sure how to categorise the mix of emotions she felt. She was simply tired, perhaps.

'That's not the same as losing your power. If it were, I wouldn't be standing here today. You saved my life with the power you say you no longer have.'

Gwyn pursed her lips and scowled at the wizard. 'If that's a roundabout way of saying "thank you" then you're welcome.'

Eldritch laughed softly, taking no offense. 'What I'm saying is that it's your access to your power that was damaged, not your power itself. With help you could learn new ways to reach it.'

'A severed spine doesn't mend just because of wishful thinking, Marcus Eldritch.'

The use of his given name was meant to needle but Eldritch let it go. 'Actually, scientists are now saying that nerve cells can regrow – but I'm sure you knew that anyway. All I meant was it's something you could work on. And if you wanted to, and if you wanted me to help, I'd be happy to do so.'

Speech over, Eldritch dropped his gaze to his hands rather than watch her face, extending her the courtesy of that small privacy. Gwyn noted the action and her exasperated huff of breath softened to more of a sigh than she was comfortable with. But, whether or not she would have told the tall wizard what she really wanted was to remain a mystery for at that moment a thin, high-pitched wail rose from the woods beyond the river. Both Gwyn and Eldritch froze and then turned as one towards the sound, listening intently.

'What the hell was that?' Eldritch was an urbanite

at heart. At ease amongst the sensory overload of the city the countryside was unfamiliar territory for him. The look he threw Gwyn held a clear request for reassurance that there was a simple, everyday explanation for what they had just heard.

'It sounded like a child. A young child.' Gwyn saw from the wizard's frown that this wasn't the comfort that Eldritch had wanted.

As the wail came again, sad and pathetic, Eldritch eyed her doubtfully. 'I haven't seen any adults around. In fact, I haven't seen anyone but us. What would a child be doing out here on its own?'

The voice did indeed sound as if its owner was too young to be out alone.

Gwyn shrugged. 'Who knows? We're not all that far from Caeglas. Kids have bikes ... they'll play anywhere. Maybe—' She stopped as the sobbing, pathetic noise punctuated her words. 'I'll say one thing: it's got good lungs on it.' Her tone was light, but she was scanning the woods as she spoke. Without conscious decision she and Eldritch moved to the far end of the bridge. 'It's going to be dark in less than an hour.' Gwyn didn't need to look at the sky or her watch to know this. She felt the imminent turning of day into night in her bones, just as she knew Eldritch did. 'I'm not the most maternal person in the world but I don't like the idea of a kid being out here on its own at this time of day. Especially one that's making that sort of noise.' She pursed her lips in an expression of resignation. 'Much though it goes against my better nature I think we'd best go and find it.'

The path on the far side of the river was less defined than the one that had brought them to the bridge. The money once provided to reclaim the old lead mining spoils had funded the initial landscaping but when it had run out the area had been left to slide quietly back into wilderness. Over time the neatly planted trees had morphed into tangled coppices: scrubby clumps of hawthorn, ash and birch, interlaced with brambles and dogwood and the waist-high stems of rosebay willowherb, standing like desiccated and brittle sentries in the lowering afternoon sun. The narrow track of flattened grass which led away from the river quickly dwindled into the merest suggestion of a pathway and soon even that vanished, leaving them uncertain as to which direction they should go. There was no sign of the child.

'Hello?' Gwyn hollered. To her relief the cry sounded again, off to their right. She scanned the undergrowth and thought she could make out the faintest impression of a track, cutting between the trees. It was little more than a badger run but it looked like the sort of trace a child might make and it went in the right direction.

She put a hand on Eldritch's arm. 'Along there, I think.'

The trees were slender-trunked but close together with thin, whippy branches which snagged on clothing and hair. Gwyn went first, sharp eyes scanning for any sign of the child, treading carefully. Underfoot the ground was choked with brambles and treacherous with rabbit scrapes and loose stones.

'Why would a kid come down here?' Eldritch put his hand up to push back a branch Gwyn had ducked under. Sometimes there were disadvantages to being tall.

'Hide and seek, maybe. If he – or she – hid too well the others might have got bored and left. Or maybe they never intended looking in the first place.' Gwyn's voice held a momentary sharpness that suggested she had had that trick played on her. 'Who knows why children do half the things they do.'

She paused and hollered again but this time there was no answering cry. She glanced at Eldritch, her raised brows asking the question she didn't put into words.

'Keep going,' he suggested. 'At least until we find out where this goes to.'

The trail, which at first had climbed gently, levelled out and then began to lead them downhill. Gradually the trees became less densely packed and they stepped out from between the last of them to find themselves on the edge of a broad hollow. Ringed in by the wooded slopes the area had a desolate, almost abandoned feel as if it had somehow been cut off and forgotten by the rest of the world.

Water filled the bottom of the hollow, a pool some thirty yards across, surrounded by a mire of noxious mud through which rusting ironwork and pieces of rotten planking stabbed upwards like the teeth of a gargantuan trap. The remaining ground was covered in couch grass and willowherb and, here and there, a shattered run of broken stone that hinted at walls long since fallen into ruin.

Gwyn eyed the scene unhappily. It had been several minutes since they had heard the last wail. 'I'm sure it was coming from this direction.'

Cautiously she and Eldritch descended the slope, picking their way over the uneven ground. In the wake of her words an uneasy silence hung over the clearing. There was no wind here and no ripples disturbed the surface of the water. Gwyn turned in a circle, scanning the surrounding trees.

'Hello?' She raised her voice further. 'Are you alright? Don't be frightened. We're here to help you.'

Together she and Eldritch listened for any response, but there was nothing to be heard. The skin prickled uneasily on the back of her neck. 'I don't like this. Something's not right.'

If Gwyn had expected an argument from the wizard, she didn't get one. Eldritch nodded, his expression troubled. 'I know what you mean,' he agreed. 'This whole place feels ...' He grappled for the right word. 'Unclean. Wrong somehow. I'm not sure what it is but something odd is going on. I hate to think of any child coming here alone.' He took a step towards the pool. 'You don't think they would have gone into the water do y— look out!'

Gwyn found herself stumbling sideways as Eldritch unceremoniously shoved her out of the way. As she went down on her knees, her hands scraping against sharp stones, she was aware of a blur of motion, of something pale charging towards them from out of the mud at the water's edge where moments before she would have sworn there had been nothing. Whatever it was it sprang at Eldritch even as the wizard was raising his arm, fingers rimmed with the blue of Levin fire. The bolt hit the leaping shape squarely – at that range it could hardly miss – but to Gwyn's amazement it had no discernible effect. The creature kept on coming, hitting Eldritch in the chest, and then there was only his plaster-wrapped arm between it and his throat. He smashed it away from him even as Gwyn prepared to fling a Levin bolt of her own, but the creature had vanished.

The wizard whirled, trying to see where it had gone. Gwyn scrambled to her feet, heart pounding as she too searched for some sign of their assailant.

'Are you okay?' Eldritch didn't break from scanning their surroundings but his voice was urgent and concerned.

'Yes, thanks to you. Nice reflexes.'

In unspoken agreement they edged together, wary, defensive and as Eldritch turned to face her, Gwyn swore. 'Sweet Lady! Look at your arm.' The cast around Eldritch's forearm showed a series of fresh white stripes where the plaster had been gouged away as if by claws. 'Are you alright?'

'For the moment.' Eldritch's face was pale, belying his own words, his grey eyes wide and shocked. 'Although that's mostly thanks to a few inches of plaster of Paris.' He too glanced at the claw marks decorating his cast. 'I don't think I'd have kept it off me otherwise.' He was silent for a moment and then added, 'You realise it absorbed my Levin bolt?' His voice was casual, his expression anything but.

Gwyn nodded. 'I saw. How is that even possible?'

'I don't know but—' The wizard's words dissolved into a curse as the creature attacked again. This time Gwyn's bolt hit an instant after Eldritch's. She knew hers couldn't match the wizard's for strength so she aimed for where she thought the thing's eyes must be. Whether that was what made the difference she couldn't have said but the combined impact knocked the creature back. It landed and darted away from them, unfeasibly swift, vanishing into the long grass, leaving Gwyn with an impression of stick-like limbs and yellow-white flesh, a too thin body and a large head crowned with clumps of long, lank hair.

'Lady bless us!' she whispered. 'I think we've found our child.'

'It's a remnant.' Eldritch's voice was clipped as he turned, trying to keep the pale shape in sight. The stands of grass shivered in its wake but, even knowing it was there, the creature was surprisingly hard to see. A glimpse of movement, a flash of pale limb and then it would vanish almost as though it were fading in and out of existence, its body slipping between dimensions. Yet the gouges on Eldritch's cast were tangible enough. 'I've never had the misfortune to face one before but that's what it is. I'm sure of it.'

'A remnant.' *Lady bless us, indeed.* Like Eldritch, Gwyn had never encountered such a thing but she knew the legends. Not so much a reanimated corpse as a body that had never been allowed to die, the spirit trapped within the flesh by a wraith from the Unseen Realm. Neither living nor dead, a remnant existed between the two worlds. It would hunt and it could kill but it wasn't truly alive. Nor yet could it die. Not while the wraith maintained control over that unnaturally preserved flesh.

'Have any children gone missing around here?'

'Not that I know of, not even in stories, but when the lead mines were open there was a whole shanty town of houses along this valley. Who knows what might have happened then.' Gwyn closed her eyes briefly and offered up a further prayer as the implication of this hit home. 'Sweet Lady!' she breathed, her voice infinitely sad. 'That's over a hundred years ago.'

A hundred years to be trapped.

Yet there was no time to be distracted by pity. Reappearing almost at their feet, the remnant leaped at them again. For an instant Gwyn was aware of a gaping mouth filled with small, pointed teeth, lunging at her face. She jerked her head back away from the snapping jaws, her arms coming up instinctively, and felt claws or teeth snag in the heavy denim of her jacket sleeve. She reached desperately for what power she could, knowing it wouldn't be enough, then blue fire exploded in front of her eyes and through the violet and white after-images she saw the child twist and leap away, untouched by a blast of Levin fire that would have been sufficient to fell a grown man.

In fact, she realised queasily, the creature wasn't just unharmed by Eldritch's bolt. If anything, it seemed more substantial than it had before. She could see it clearly where it crouched close to the ruin of a wall only a few yards in front of them.

The remnant might once have been a child but now it was a shape out of nightmare: it's thin, naked body androgynous, the skin moist and glistening with a pallid phosphorescence, sickly pale as a corpse and hanging over the bones as though the flesh beneath had melted away. Long skeletal fingers were tipped with thick, talon-like nails. Dark eyes stared unblinking from large orbits in the misshapen skull. Revulsion made Gwyn want to turn away. Self-preservation kept her focussed on it as it started to circle.

It moved fluidly, unhurried but purposeful, gliding over the uneven ground and Gwyn and Eldritch turned with it like deer facing a wolf. When it stopped Gwyn felt a small thrill of fear as she realised it was now between them and the path they had followed into the hollow. The thought of trying to make it up that slope while the remnant tore at their flesh made her shudder but she was conscious that with the water at their backs there was no retreat in that direction either.

'It seems it doesn't want us to leave.' Eldritch's softly spoken words summed up Gwyn's fears.

'No, and if it's absorbing our power I can understand why. I had no idea remnants could do that.'

'Me neither. Unfortunately, no one's bothered to tell it that.' Eldritch wiped sweat from his face with his good hand but his eyes never left the remnant. 'At a guess it's using the energy to become more corporeal.'

'It's already able to hurt us,' Gwyn snapped, though she had reached the same conclusion. 'How much more physical does it need to be?'

But for once the wizard had no answer. 'Perhaps that's why it lured us down here,' he said instead. 'One hundred years is a long time to hold a body together.'

'But if it's been here so long why has no one seen it before now? The demon's avatar was manifesting for barely a quarter of that time and you know how many Black Dog legends and sightings sprang out of that. Yet I don't know of a single local story about a White Child.'

'Who knows? There was an awful lot of power flying around when Aidan and I fought the demon. Maybe when the boundary closed something else shifted. It wasn't the most controlled of circumstances.' Eldritch nodded ruefully at his plaster cast. After a moment he added, 'It scarcely matters. We're the ones who are going to have to deal with it.'

The weary resignation in the wizard's tone had Gwyn risking a longer look at her companion. What she saw didn't fill her with confidence in their ability to deal with anything. Eldritch's face had gone beyond pale to ashen and from the way he was now cradling his right arm close to his body Gwyn guessed it was hurting damnably.

She hoped he hadn't re-broken the bones of his wrist when he had batted the remnant away. Not that there was anything that could be done about it now.

The wizard swayed slightly or maybe, Gwyn thought, she was the one doing the swaying. Her head ached fiercely and she was aware that everything had the brittle sharpness that came when she had overused her power. Neither she nor the wizard would be able to keep this up for long.

She took a deliberate steadying breath, letting it out as a sigh. 'If we can't use power against it, we need to do something different.'

'I'm open to suggestions.'

'We'll have to stop it physically.'

'With what, our bare hands?' Eldritch laughed but the sound was devoid of humour. 'I can't see that working.'

Gwyn bristled. 'Well,' she snapped, 'we're going to have to do something.'

'We are.' Eldritch squared his shoulders decisively, visibly pushing back his fatigue. 'I can hold it off while you make a break for it.'

Anger brought Gwyn a welcome spurt of energy. 'Oh, don't be melodramatic. I refuse to be beaten by something the size of an average four-year-old.'

'Most four-year-olds don't have claws that can rip

through plaster of Paris,' Eldritch said, pointedly.

'You obviously haven't done enough babysitting,' Gwyn muttered. 'Lady knows, there are plenty of reasons why I don't like children.' But in the back of her mind an idea was beginning to form.

'Wraiths might be able to keep death at bay but they're not invincible. From the moment they take over a physical body they're fighting to maintain it. They do it very well but if we can cause the remnant a catastrophic injury – something the wraith can't easily heal – there's a chance we can break its hold. It will have to let go of the body.' At least, that was her understanding of remnant lore. She took the wizard's silence as agreement and ploughed on. 'It's obvious that throwing power is getting us nowhere. I know you can throw pain, but can you throw anything else?'

'Such as?'

'How about compassion?'

'What?'

Under other circumstances Gwyn might have laughed at the wizard's incomprehension.

Well, that answers that question.

Clearly, he couldn't. She would have to do it herself then ... if she could.

She pushed her hair back from her face and wished she didn't feel quite so queasy. Yet it wasn't her ability to throw the emotion that concerned her so much as her capacity to feel it in the first place. Could she have compassion for something that was trying to kill them, compassion for something that she herself was going to try to destroy?

Lady help me, she thought. But perhaps she could. She was no saint, yet she wouldn't retaliate if a frightened animal lashed out at her. Likewise, it had been compassion that had made her stop on the way home from Aberystwyth the previous week and deal with the rabbit she had seen hit by the car in front of her. She had picked the injured animal from the road as gently as she could and then she had broken its neck. There had been nothing she could do for it and no way she could have left it there to die slowly and in pain.

Surely, she could feel compassion for a remnant child trapped on the borders of death for over a century. If she couldn't then what she was about to try was likely to get her and Eldritch killed. The realisation brought a rueful grimace but no change of mind: it wasn't as though they had any other options.

'Alright,' she said, consciously turning her thoughts away from what she was about to do. 'I think this will work, but you need to be ready with every ounce of power you can manage.'

'Okay.' Eldritch waited but when she didn't

volunteer any further details he asked, 'Are you going to tell me the plan or do I have to guess?'

'I'd rather not, just in case that thing can pick the thoughts out of our heads. You'll know when it's the right time.'

'Oh, good.' The wizard's tone was dry as the Sahara.

Gwyn almost smiled. 'Eldritch—' She stopped, not sure whether she should be apologising or explaining. 'If this doesn't work things are going to get nasty.'

'I'd already guessed that much.' There was the hint of a feral grin in Eldritch's response. 'It's going to get nasty if we don't do anything. I've got your back, Gwyn,' he added. 'Always.'

'Let's hope it doesn't come to that.'

In front of them the remnant was moving again. It circled a few steps to the left and then made a short, darting feint, almost as though trying to draw their fire, before sidling back. All the time it was watching them through those dark, unblinking eyes. Watching and assessing, Gwyn thought, judging the strength of its prey. It was time to change the game.

Keeping her eyes on the remnant, Gwyn knelt, bringing herself down to its level. She felt Eldritch shift to stand over her. 'Okay.' She barely breathed the reassurance at him as she readied herself. 'Let's do this.'

Compassion. The willingness to be present in the face of suffering. This child had suffered horribly – was still suffering, Gwyn reminded herself. She might not have the details, but she knew enough: that the child had strayed from safety into the very borderlands of death. Terrified and alone, perhaps desperately crying for help – how long had it been before it had realised that no one would come? Gwyn opened herself to that understanding. She shivered as a cold, aching weariness seeped into her heart and she felt tears that weren't her own building in her eyes. Yes, Gwyn thought, she could find compassion for such a creature. She wove that understanding like the warp and weft of a gossamer shawl, set to wrap around the shoulders of a frightened child, and pushed the feeling out into the air in front of her.

She was aware, almost as if she were watching the scene at a distance, that the remnant had stopped its predatory circling and crouched down, its thin body hunching low to the ground. She heard Eldritch's hiss of breath, felt her own heartbeat hitch as the remnant's muscles bunched in preparation for a leap and then, just as abruptly, it pulled back.

'Easy,' she murmured, not sure which of them she was reassuring. 'Easy.' She conjured stillness and peace and the warm comfort of being held in loving arms.

Easy. Easy.

She sent her thoughts out, a gentle spiderweb to catch and contain, and the monstrosity in front of her swayed backwards and forwards in time with her breath.

Carefully, carefully Gwyn reached towards it with her senses. There was confusion: an inhuman need to rend and kill pitted against a desire for something else that was barely understood. Attracted and repelled in equal measure, the creature wavered, its desires teetering on a knife edge and Gwyn could not tell which way it would go. Then the remnant took a half step forward.

It wasn't an attack but nor was it a submission and Gwyn found herself struggling against a conflict of her own. She had to believe in the child, yet it was hard to see past the remnant's warped physicality when her senses were filled with the wet leather slither of moist and glistening skin and the sickly-sour smell emanating from that unrotten flesh.

She needed a name, she thought, something tangible to link to. Swallowing revulsion and fear, she pushed back against the overwhelming sense of wrongness.

You can do this. You can.

Opening deeper she reached again, seeking the faint threads of memory that trailed from the remnant's flesh, letting them slide over her. The distant echo of a woman's voice sounded in her ears.

Brangwen.

She heard the name called, sweet and light, and the memory of a kiss brushed her skin. There were soft arms that rocked her until sleep came, arms which carried the warm smells of baking, of clean washing and the summer sun. There were other arms too: strong ones that held her, tossing her in the air until she giggled, the male scent of sweat and soap enveloping her. The memories were there, of love and safety, but the remnant child no longer understood what those things meant.

'Oh, Brangwen *bach*,' Gwyn murmured. She focussed on the little girl she could see in her mind's eye rather than the monstrosity that faced her. 'Little white raven. Come here, love.'

The remnant hung back but Gwyn poured compassion into the link she had forged between them and slowly it edged towards her, drawn by a power it could not resist. Closer and closer it came. The hands with those terrible talons reached out towards her. Heedless of the danger Gwyn reached out in return. She heard Eldritch's breath snag as she drew the remnant into her arms and hugged it to her, yet the wizard made no move to intervene. Eldritch trusted she knew what she was doing. Taking comfort from that unspoken support Gwyn emersed herself fully in the link and addressed the child held captive in the remnant's flesh.

'It's time to go home, little one.' She cupped a hand to the remnant's cold cheek and looked into those huge, unblinking eyes. 'You're a child of the light, Brangwen.' With all the power remaining to her she reached for that life spark within the child, reinforcing the connection. 'Whatever has happened you can never be anything else. You know where you should be.'

Leaning forward she planted a kiss on the cold, white forehead. Her fingers slid through the lank hair to frame the curve of the misshapen skull. 'Lady bless you, Brangwen.' She spoke to the image of the little girl she could see so clearly. Then she drove her right hand up and inwards, punching it towards her left palm with all the strength she could muster, so that the pointed chunk of stone clenched in her fist smashed into the remnant's temple, crushing through it as though it were an eggshell.

Even as the remnant's body spasmed Gwyn threw it away from her with a small sob, sickened and revolted as seething black smoke poured from the corpse.

'Now!' she screamed and in that same instant Eldritch's Levin fire scorched into the writhing mass, catching it and the small body and enveloping them in one searing ball of fire. Gwyn threw her own power into the inferno as well, feeding it with all the loathing and disgust she felt, not so much for the remnant but for the wraith that had stolen a child's body and for what she had been forced to do to destroy that malevolent parasite. Only when a wave of blackness passed across her vision and her power faltered and stuttered, drained down to its dregs, did she stop. By then there was nothing in front of her but a pile of soft white ash.

For a long moment nothing moved in the clearing. Then slowly Eldritch folded to his knees beside her.

'Dear God.' He looked from Gwyn to the ashes and then back, staring at her as though he had never seen her before. 'You smashed its head in.'

Gwyn dropped her head, unwilling to meet his gaze. 'It was the only thing I could do.' She shuddered and scrubbed her palms against her jeans as though by doing so she might wipe away the kinaesthetic memory of what she had just done. 'Sometimes a clean death is the kindest thing you can offer.' Another shudder racked her. 'I couldn't heal her.' It was true but that didn't make it any more palatable. 'At least this way she's finally at peace.'

She stopped wiping her palms on her thighs and hugged her arms round herself instead. After a moment, Eldritch laid an awkward hand on her shoulder. They knelt there, not speaking, not looking at each other, and the first trace of wind they had felt within the hollow stirred the ashes. Little by little the breeze picked apart the small pile, whirling the fragments into the air and scattering them until there was nothing left to show what had happened.

It was Eldritch who moved first. Levering himself up, with the stiffness of a man twice his age, he stood swaying for a moment until he found his balance. Then he extended his left hand to Gwyn. She took it gratefully, not sure she could have risen unaided. For a moment the pair of them clung together before Gwyn took a half step back. She offered the wizard a tentative smile. 'Thank you.'

Eldritch's eyebrows raised as if to ask which part of the afternoon's activities she was thanking him for. Then he shrugged. 'Any time. Although maybe not right at this moment,' he amended. 'I don't know about you, but I don't have enough energy left to magic my way out of a paper bag. Can we go home now?'

Gwyn studied the wizard. He looked as beaten up as she felt. Fine demon hunters, the pair of them. But they had survived. A trace of mischief stirred in her eyes. 'In that case ... how about a game of Pooh Sticks?'

ABOUT 'THE REMNANT CHILD'

Readers familiar with my *Dark Places* novels will recognise

Eldritch and Gwyn. This story takes place three or four weeks after the events depicted in *The Demon's Call* and *Child of the Covenant,* as Gwyn and Eldritch are recovering from the injuries they sustained during those adventures.

You can read the first chapter of *To Pay for the Crossing* – the latest *Dark Places* novel – in the back pages of this book.

15

THE NEW COAT

I got a new coat today. Dad gave it to me. I didn't ask where it came from. It's bright blue, like the sky at midsummer or the colour of Mum's eyes. The pockets are deep so I can put my hands in them to keep them warm and there's a fur trim around the hood. My new coat's just like the one Sasha, my best friend, has.

When I saw her wearing it for the first time, I really wanted one too, not because it looked so much warmer than my coat – although it did – but because if we had the same it would be like we were twins. People used to laugh at how alike we were, because our hair was long and straight and the same sort of blonde. Often, we'd plait it the same way and people who didn't know us would ask if we really were sisters. We'd laugh and pretend it was true.

I haven't seen Sasha since the bad men came to our village. I think her parents took her and her brothers further down the mountain. A lot of people decided to go that way. They said it was the only thing to do with the winter snows already here. I like to think that Sasha's coat will be keeping her warm now, wherever she is.

We didn't go with the rest of the village when they left. Mum and Dad talked about it for a long time. Mum's dad was a trapper; he was happy being in the mountains throughout the winter. He even used to take Mum out with him when she was just a little older than I am now. Dad said that too many people on the roads would be a target. He agreed we'd be safer in the old caves that Grandad had talked about so that's where we went.

The snow was deep, and it was hard to walk through it. I got so cold I couldn't feel my feet, but I tried to keep going. I didn't complain but Dad must have known because after a while he picked me up and carried me even though he was carrying his big rucksack too. It was a long way to the caves. I don't think anyone but Mum or Dad could have found them. Sometimes I imagine Grandad bringing Mum here as a little girl. I wonder if she had a coat like mine to keep her warm.

I love my new coat. There's a hole in it, but I don't mind as it's in the back, so it doesn't show once I've put it on. There's a bit of a stain around the hole too, but I pretended not to notice and didn't say anything. I'd seen Mum rubbing it with snow trying to get it clean and I didn't want to seem ungrateful. I think of Sasha a lot when I'm wearing my new coat. I don't think I'll ever see her again.

ABOUT 'THE NEW COAT'

This story was prompted by the song 'You Stay Here' by Richard Shindell. Richard sings his songs from many points of view; 'You Stay Here' comes from the perspective of a refugee in the hills of Srebrenica.

Children are often more perceptive than adults give them credit for. I felt the lines 'We'll wash them clean with melted snow. The kids don't ever have to know.' might be wishful thinking on the part of the adult narrator.

While Richard's song takes place during the Bosnian Conflict of the 1990s, my story is set in a dystopian future that I hope will remain unrealised.

16

FAMILIAR PROBLEMS

There were good reasons why witches had cats, Mercy concluded. For one thing, they didn't mind heights, which was always a plus when it came to flying. They exhibited natural balance and poise but, perhaps more importantly, even wet through – and most cats of Mercy's acquaintance refused to get wet – they didn't weigh anything approaching forty pounds.

She looked at the sad remains of her broom and the large Bernese Mountain Dog sat sheepishly amidst the wreckage. It hadn't been Sophie's fault – not exactly – but when just over three stone of dog spots something exciting mid-flight and tries to dive off the broom and give chase, well, even with a safety harness the resulting load shift has catastrophic consequences for one's aerodynamics.

Mercy sighed. She was going to be the laughing-stock of the coven if news of this got out. She could already imagine the rolled eyes and the sniggers behind her back, not to mention the dressing down she was sure to receive from the head witch. Her shoulders hunched reflexively. The words *I'm only saying this for your own good* were as blood-curdling as any curse when accompanied by that all-knowing, tight-lipped smile. Mercy was sure the woman was keeping a log of her misdemeanours.

No, there really was only one thing for it. She would have to put this right before anyone noticed. Taking a deep breath, she pulled herself up to her full, if modest, height and raised her wand.

'Hold still, darling. This won't hurt a bit.'

Mercy crossed her fingers behind her back.

Hopefully!

The blinding flash of light was accompanied by a fleeting whiff of rosemary and the sweet scent of cake batter. Mercy blinked furiously to clear her watering eyes and reminded herself that she must remember her goggles when next she came to cast a transformation spell. Her face tingled with what felt like a bad case of sunburn but with luck she hadn't singed her eyebrows off this time around.

Oh, this had better have worked!

Steeling herself for failure, she looked at the results of her casting. Her broom remained in pieces but where there had previously been a large dog there was now a petite tortoiseshell cat. It gave her a vexed stare then turned its back and fastidiously began to wash one paw.

Mercy smothered a grin as she reholstered her wand. Problem solved.

ABOUT 'FAMILIAR PROBLEMS'

A friend's broken arm – and the reason for it – inspired this very short story. Names have been changed to protect the innocent.

About the Author

Kim Gravell lives a dangerous life which is to say she has a compulsive writing habit that leads her to spend more time than is healthy sat in front of her PC. This has resulted in a variety of short stories published in various magazines and anthologies and three paranormal adventure novels, two of which – *The Demon's Call* and *To Pay for the Crossing* – have won Red Ribbons in the Wishing Shelf book awards.

Kim lives in mid-Wales with her husband and their two rescue cats. She loves travelling, people watching and animals of all shapes and sizes and can no more imagine spending a day without writing than she could a day without breathing.

To find out more about Kim's writing visit her website:
www.kimgravell.com

Read on for an extract from
To Pay For The Crossing

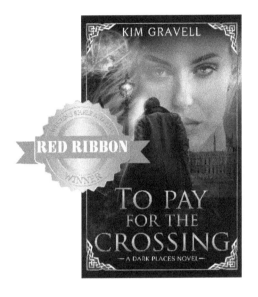

The latest novel in the award-winning *Dark Places* series of paranormal adventures.

Available now

The demon was gone.

Kneeling in the middle of his living room, Marcus Eldritch knew that he had won. Yet the thought gave him no satisfaction. What he had achieved felt more like defeat than victory.

Helen was dead.

It scarcely mattered that she had been dead since the moment the demon had possessed her, her body reduced to a shell in which the demon could exist in the Mortal World. While it had occupied her there had been the chance to pretend that the woman he loved was still alive. Even after he had realised the truth, when he knew he was only deceiving himself, still there had been times when he would glance at her and, just for a moment, let himself believe he was wrong. She had been his soulmate, his other half. How could she be dead when he could see her there in front of him? But he knew the truth, and, with that realisation, there was no going back.

So, he had armoured himself for the battle he knew was inevitable. There had been no place for grief, no time to mourn for all he had lost. He had locked his emotions away behind a façade and played the demon at its own game. All he allowed himself to feel was a cold, focused anger that sustained him, carried him through as he laid his plans, kept him going until the molten fire of battle took over. Now, even that was gone. He felt as hollow as the shell the demon had left behind, reamed out and empty. The demon was dead. Helen was dead. Now his task was finished, and he could die too.

Eldritch lifted his head and looked at his wife's body. Stretched beside him, her face peaceful, Helen might have been sleeping. The final welter of Levin bolts that had driven the demon from her had left no mark on her body. She looked as though she might wake at the slightest touch. Without conscious thought, Eldritch stretched his fingers towards her cheek, where a blush of colour still warmed the skin, and froze. His breath seemed to congeal in his lungs. Surely the universe could have spared him this? His gut twisted and bile rose in his throat. He had thought he had reached the nadir of his despair, but it seemed there was a wealth of pain yet awaiting him. Helen was still breathing.

A man unfamiliar with demonic possession might have rejoiced, but Eldritch was a wizard and he knew the bitter truth. Those who had been possessed did not recover. Usually, a host's body would die when the possessing demon was driven out, but not always. Sometimes the body continued – an empty shell that went on functioning, devoid of the spirit that had lived within it, purposeless and without hope of recovery. It was the cruellest twist; Helen was dead even though her body still lived.

Eldritch wasn't sure how long he knelt there. His hands tangled in Helen's hair, running the corn-silk fineness of it through his fingers like a man praying over the beads of a rosary, while his mind stalled, caught in a maelstrom of images of all he had lost. When he came back to himself the light had faded from the windows and the room was sunk into shadows, but he knew what he would do.

He pulled Helen's body into his arms, cradling the warm weight of her against his chest. He inhaled her scent, felt the slow rise and fall of her breath, and his heart broke anew. 'Forgive me.'

His muscles cried out in protest as he lurched upright and carried her to the settee, lowering her down carefully onto the cream leather and positioning a cushion beneath her head, as though such niceties could make a difference now.

Moving mechanically, he circled the room, drawing the curtains and switching on a table lamp to hold back the dusk. He chose a favourite CD and slid it into the player. Finally, as the first notes of the piano tumbled into the air, he knelt and lit the gas fire. For several heartbeats he stared into the flames, letting that ancient practice steady him. Then, calling his power to him, he reached out and blocked the fire's air intake. The flames trembled then steadied, their colour shifting from blue to an orangey yellow. Eldritch watched them until he was certain the fire would continue to burn. There would be no explosion to endanger anyone else. Even now that was important to him. All he wanted was the slow build-up of carbon monoxide wrapping around him and Helen, ensuring that they would sleep forever in each other's arms.

Returning to the settee, he knelt once more beside his wife's still form. Helen's lips were slightly parted as if she might whisper to him, but her periwinkle blue eyes were closed and they would never open again. Tenderly, Eldritch kissed those closed lids. He brushed the hair back from her forehead and kissed her once more, cupping her cheeks and staring down at her, filling his mind with her image.

'I love you,' he whispered. 'Wait for me.'

Then he lay down, wrapping his arms around her and drawing her body close. Closing his eyes, he waited for death to claim him.

Milton Keynes UK
Ingram Content Group UK Ltd.
UKHW040335141124
451090UK00005B/154

9 781916 324725